Ben Okri has published many books including *The Famished Road*, which won the Booker Prize in 1991, *Songs of Enchantment, Dangerous Love* and his latest novel *Infinite Riches*. He has also published two books of poems, the most recent being *Mental Fight*, and a collection of non-fiction, *A Way of Being Free*. He has been a Fellow Commoner in Creative Arts, at Trinity College, Cambridge and he is a Fellow of the Royal Society of Literature.

Ben Okri's books have won several awards including the Commonwealth Writers Prize for Africa, the *Paris Review* Aga Khan Prize for Fiction, the Chianti Rufino-Antico Fattore International Literary Prize and the Premio Grinzane Cavour Prize. He is a vice-president of the English Centre of International PEN and was presented with the Crystal Award for outstanding contribution to the Arts and to cross-cultural understanding by the World Economic Forum. In addition, the University of Westminster awarded him an Honorary Doctorate of Literature. Ben Okri was born in Minna, Nigeria and lives in London.

'In this powerful, sensuous and philosophical book, I saw universal aspects of the human condition like loneliness, joy, survival, despair, courage, oblivion, pain, terror, optimism and knowledge ... Okri's use of language is beautifully, thrillingly and vibrantly poetic. Smiles can be heard; silences have melodies; sounds have colours and tenderness has a fragrance ... You will probably be as enchanted, intellectually challenged and moved (almost to tears) as I was' *European*

'A compassionate voice, gently spoken and full of wonder, yet alert and dynamic' *Sunday Times*

'Here we have a pilgrimage of the soul that is both graceful and enigmatic.

Astonishing the Gods starts with a nameless man, born invisible, who embarks on a quest to discover if there is more to his life than this. He is entranced by an island where he, in turn, can only sense the presence of the inhabitants. This realm of the marvellous – the avenue of mirrors (where each traveller sees something different), the bridge made of mist – is explored with a series of spirit guides who belong to a higher civilisation that has learnt from its terrible past how to refine what they value into invisibility.

Along the way our pilgrim re-learns much: discovery is made harder by attempts to define; rejecting the negative is the first step – "It is only mystery that keeps things alive." ... Okri's fable of restoration and belonging is oddly compelling, largely owing to his Borgesian short sentences and the visual elements of his oneiric prose ... a philosophical romance ... exciting, like a trip into a de Chirico landscape ... You have to read it to believe it' *Daily Telegraph*

'*Astonishing the Gods* is a new creation myth ... a hymn to the richness and the potential of all the invisible people everywhere. all the unwritten worlds ... Ben Okri's fifth novel and his mos removed and fabulist yet, is an empowering fable of the quest for identity ... Okri's concern has been to reveal the "myths and magic in the air" of the ordinary world; this tale of paradoxes ... enacts the rituals of storytelling to produce, at once ironically and hopefully, a new belief system, one that's a fusion of pagan and Christian expectations, and one with a prophetic force ... This is Okri's achievement, the making of an imaginative space for the invisible forgotten peoples. It's a beautiful book ... its mere task to make the impossible possible'
Scotsman

'*Astonishing the Gods* is properly worked and exact, and fulfils Calvino's prescription for lightness – being like a bird, rather than a feather ...

This novel is like a forbiddingly high-sided mountainous pass ... Reaching it is a rare achievement ... This is an impressive, brave and often beautiful little book'
New Statesman & Society

Astonishing the Gods

BEN OKRI

PHŒNIX

A PHOENIX PAPERBACK

First published in Great Britain by Phoenix House in 1995
This paperback edition published in 1996 by Phoenix,
an imprint of Orion Books Ltd,
Orion House, 5 Upper St Martin's Lane,
London WC2H 9EA

Reissued 1999

A CIP catalogue record for this book
is available from the British Library.

Printed and bound in Great Britain by
Clays Ltd, St Ives plc

BOOK ONE

BOOK ONE

One

It is better to be invisible. His life was better when he was invisible, but he didn't know it at the time.

He was born invisible. His mother was invisible too, and that was why she could see him. His people lived contented lives, working on the farms, under the familiar sunlight. Their lives stretched back into the invisible centuries and all that had come down from those differently coloured ages were legends and rich traditions, unwritten and therefore remembered. They were remembered because they were lived.

He grew up without contradiction in the sunlight of the unwritten ages, and as a boy he dreamt of becoming a shepherd. He was sent to school, where he learnt strange notions, odd alphabets, and where he discovered that time can be written down in words.

It was in books that he first learnt of his invisibility. He searched for himself and his people in all the history books he read and discovered to his youthful astonishment that he didn't exist. This troubled him so much that he resolved, as soon as he was old enough, to leave his land and find the people who did exist, to see what they looked like.

He kept this discovery of his recent invisibility to himself and soon forgot his dream of becoming a shepherd. But in the end he didn't have to wait till he was old enough. One night when the darkness was such that it confirmed his invisibility in the universe, he fled from home, ran to the nearest port, and stole off across the emerald sea.

He travelled for seven years. He did all the jobs that came his way. He learnt many languages. He learnt many kinds of silences. He kept his mouth shut as much as possible and listened to all the things that men and nature had to say. He travelled many seas and saw many cities and witnessed many kinds of evil that can sprout from the hearts of men. He travelled the seas, saying little, and when anyone asked him why he journeyed and what his destination was, he always gave two answers. One answer was for the ear of his questioner. The second answer was for his own heart. The first answer went like this:

'I don't know why I am travelling. I don't know where I am going.'

And the second answer went like this:

'I am travelling to know why I am invisible. My quest is for the secret of visibility.'

Those who worked with him in those years saw him as a simple man. Actually, they didn't see him at all.

Two

After travelling for seven years he arrived at a strange port. The town seemed empty. The houses were silent. He disembarked and found himself in a great square patterned in black and white, as if it were a giant chessboard. The air was tinged with an orange glow. There was an eternal motionlessness about everything that made him feel he had wandered into a disquieting dream.

The town was empty, but he could feel that there were people all around. He fancied he heard an occasional whisper in the air. He was so disturbed by the strangeness of the town that he wandered deeper into its riddle. But the town was a riddle without an answer. Everywhere he heard tinkling bells. Happy voices laughed in the gentle wind. Even their laughter was a kind of secret. In the far corner of the square he heard sweet voices reciting the ineffable names of things. He was so overcome with the invisible enchantments of the town that he didn't want to leave.

He had been following the musical voices of young girls whispering unseen beneath the flavoured moonlight of that mysterious town, when he heard the blasts from the ship calling him to return. The moonlight, glowing on the chessboard patterns of the town's magnificent square, filled his heart with a beautiful solitude that would haunt him for the rest of his life.

As he turned to go, tearing himself unwillingly from the limpid voices of the girls, he was suddenly touched with the scent of honeysuckle. He started to weep. A haunting sonata, yellow and lilac amongst the dazzling illusions of the quivering chessboard, started up far behind him. He wept as he listened to the flute melodies piping out forgotten moments of his life.

He was still weeping when a gentle voice, out of the fragrant air, said:

'Why are your crying?'

He started. Not seeing who was addressing him, but not overly disturbed by it, he replied:

'I am weeping because I don't understand the beauty of this island.'

'Then why don't you stay?'

'But how can I stay? I can't see the inhabitants. I don't even know where I am.'

'You shouldn't worry. The inhabitants can't see you either. At least most of them can't. You are just a voice to me. But everything is in your voice. Besides, you are seeking something that you've already found, but you don't know it. Such are the causes of unhappiness.'

'Where is this place?'

'It doesn't have a name. We don't believe in names. Names have a way of making things disappear.'

'I don't understand.'

'When you name something it loses its existence to you. Things die a little when we name them. I am speaking only of this island. I cannot speak for anywhere else.'

'So if you don't want things to disappear what do you do?'

'We think of them. We dwell in them. We let them dwell in us. You ask many questions: if you are so interested why

6

don't you stay and live with us and learn our mysteries?'

'Thank you, but my ship is calling me. I must set sail, or I will never find the things that made me leave my homeland.'

'You may learn much here.'

'But I may never catch another ship again. I don't know how frequently they come here. And then I would miss the sea and the journey.'

'The sea is always there, ships come when they will, the journey always continues, but this island is discovered only once in a lifetime – if you're lucky.'

The ship's blast sounded again, calling three times in stern warning. He shuddered at the sound. When the third blast fell silent, he listened to the plaintive wind. He listened to the flute choruses threading the cypress trees. He listened to the sound of water flowing among the wreaths of acanthus leaves in the marble fountain.

Lost in wonder, he stared at the white harmonic buildings round the square. He noticed their pure angles, their angelic buttresses, and their columns of gleaming marble. He inhaled the fragrance of childhood, of sweet yellow melodies, and of ripening mangoes. When a woman's voice began singing from the spire of the blue temple of that land, the wind itself became silent. He noticed how all things invisible seemed to become attentive to the glorious singing which poured a golden glow into the limpid moonlight. He found himself smiling. When the singing stopped, and a new happy silence lingered, he decided to stay.

Three

The ship set sail without him. He watched as it rocked its way over the green waters. The port was still deserted and all over that island the silence became deeper. As the ship disappeared over the horizon, time changed around him. Slowly, he ceased to be aware of himself. One moment he was in the middle of the shimmering chessboard square, and the next moment he found himself wandering over streets of polished glass, wandering through alleys paved as if with stained-glass windows. Light poured upwards from below, as if the island's relationship with the moon and sky had become inverted.

The voice that was his guide was silent; it was only the instinct of another presence which calmed him as he walked through the serenity of the island.

He was struck by the buildings. They were magnificent; they were bold; they had astounding facades, with stately columns and conch-shell capitals and graceful entablatures. The pedestals displayed a lofty and balanced sense of proportion. The buildings, all apparently empty, loomed everywhere. They attracted the lights, they gave off an air of grandeur and majesty, and yet they seemed to hang in midspace. They appeared to rest on nothing, suspended. Even the great churches, with their golden domes and their moody spires, seemed to be made of an ethereal substance. The buildings, in their perfection, looked like some kind of dream-created illusion. He was puzzled by the monumentality of things and their apparent lightness.

He came to the wonderful avenue of mirrors. The house-fronts, the castle facades, the bridges, the villas, the basilicas, were all made of mirrors. The mysterious loggias where statues stared at him with an almost palpable longing and lust were also made of mirrors. They all reflected themselves into an oddly terrifying infinity. When he saw how all things multiplied everything else, multiplying him wherever he looked, he experienced the strangest sensation. It was a sense of the happiness he must have known before birth, a happiness that he suspected was his eternal birthright. It reminded him obliquely of the joy he experienced when he first saw a rainbow. And while he lingered in that mood he noticed a rainbow gradually materialise over the golden dome of the silent church. The rainbow, reflected in all the mirrors of the castles and housefronts, had clear colours of such astonishing beauty, complementing the calm radiance of the moon, that he found himself saying:

'You must be masters of the art of happiness.'

The voice guiding him laughed a little. Then fell silent. Then said:

'We are masters of the art of transcendence. We are masters of suffering. I'd appreciate it if you never mention the word happiness on this island again.'

Four

The avenue of mirrors seemed to go on forever. As he went along, shivering in the silver facades, he felt himself becoming more insubstantial, less real. He seemed to be losing his identity to the mirrors. He felt as if the heaviest and least important parts of him were dissolving in the effulgent lights. At the same time he felt himself becoming more peaceful, less questing, and freer from anxieties. He would normally have been quite afraid to lose such a familiar part of himself as his anxieties. But he was much too preoccupied with the brilliance of the lights. He was fascinated by the way they changed, the way they flared in red and gold. He was mesmerised by the gyrating spectacle of an infinity of perfect realms, perfect interiors, pure landscapes of joy, and the atmosphere of bliss that dwelt in the shining depths of the mirrors.

To his astonishment, as he looked deeper into the mirrors, as into the depths of a magical lake, he saw beautiful women playing mandolins, reading illuminated books, singing silently in chorus, reciting words that turned into radiant colours, dancing naked on lacquered floors. White and yellow birds circled them overhead in the spacious air of their palaces made from moonlight.

He was about to speak when another wonderful sight caught his eyes. He turned and beheld, in another mirror, a magnificent garden in which flowers bathed in a celestial glow. As he watched, entranced, a white unicorn with an emerald horn trotted past gracefully, scattering enchanted beams of beatification.

Further on, in the blue mirrors fronting the Great Basilica of Truth, he saw a green lake. In the middle of the emerald lake, focal point of all the magic lights, was the forgotten sword of Justice. Its blade was of incorruptible gold, and it pointed to the illuminated heavens, dazzling the eye with its divine purity.

'I understand nothing,' he said.

He hadn't recovered from the wonders he had just seen. He never would.

'Retain your bewilderment,' said the voice, his guide. 'Your bewilderment will serve you well.'

'But what do all these things mean?'

'What do you mean by mean?'

'Who are the beautiful women? What does that wonderful unicorn signify? What is the sword?'

The voice said:

'You will meet the women later, the unicorn is seen only by those who can see it, and the sword is the sword.'

'I still don't understand.'

'Things are what they are. That is their power. They are all the things we think they are, all the things we sense they are, and more. They are themselves. If they meant something they would be less. Whatever you see is your personal wealth and paradise. You're lucky if you can see wonderful things. Some people who have been here see only infernal things. What you see is what you are, or what you will become. Many of our greatest men and women have been here for hundreds of years and have never seen the unicorn. You have just arrived and you have seen it.'

The voice paused. Then after a while, with a little amused laughter, he said:

'The council will be delighted by this. The royal astrologers who predicted this moment will be overjoyed. Without knowing it, we have been awaiting your arrival for a long time. If you survive what is to come, if you make it to the great convocation, it is possible that you are the one who will initiate the new cycle of the Invisibles.'

Towards the end of the street he saw angels taking flight in the last mirrors. They had rainbow wings. The upward rush of their lights, their mighty glowing presence, terrified him and almost made his heart stop. His terror momentarily blinded him. It was a long while before he could breath normally again and resume his journey into the island.

Five

After the flight of the angels, he did not feel quite the same. He wasn't sure what had changed, but he felt as if he were at an angle inside himself. The sudden sight of the angels seemed to have twisted his neck in some obscure way. Besides, after their heavenly brilliance had passed, the world seemed a little darker.

He had entered another marvellous street. The moonlight made the chessboard universe quiver. At first, as he went down the street, he noticed huge white and silver forms looming high up in the air. He noticed the great extensions of their dazzling and partially concealed forms. They filled him with an unaccountably holy terror. The forms, alive in a way that only the most awesome things are alive, encompassed him with their total knowledge of his being. As he passed under them, he became even lighter. He felt himself changing into light.

The huge white forms above were recomposing him as he passed beneath their blinding radiance. They transformed him subtly. They re-ordered his being. Into the holes that terror had opened in him, they seemed to pour a dizzying understanding of all the nameless things he would need to know when he would need to know them.

It struck him that he was being filled to bursting with future knowledge and with joy enough to last all the darkness that was to come. He had no way of explaining it, but as he passed beneath the vast wings of the brilliant forms – radiating light like a new star – he seemed to feel an understanding of things before his time, beyond his time, beyond his life and quest, an understanding that flowed through from all the past and future ages.

As he went he heard strange whisperings within him, as if many voices in code were reciting, gently, into his heart and spirit, all the secret laws of known and unknown universes.

He had always thought himself invisible. He had always thought that invisibility was the worst thing that could befall a person or a people. But as he went under the beautiful power of the radiant wings hovering between earth and star, it occurred to him that he was becoming more invisible than he had ever known before, more invisible than he ever suspected was possible.

It frightened him that there were gradations of invisibility, gradations and depths. His mind spun in the pure horror of this notion. He felt himself sinking into those depths as he passed beneath the charged immanent wings. And as he sank deeper into new invisibilities he had a sudden monstrous suspicion of the endlessness of it, the bottomlessness of it, till he could imagine a stage of invisibility that shaded into the eternal, the infinite.

At that point his mind plunged into total darkness. He found himself spinning in that darkness. Then he felt himself falling, falling away from himself, falling without end into a darkness that got deeper and more unbearable. The only thing he could do to rescue himself from the sheer terror of his internal abyss was to scream. He screamed in absolute horror of becoming more invisible than he already was. So loud and so piercingly did he scream that the entire island seemed to resound with it. After a while he wasn't sure if it was him or if it was the universe that was screaming. He felt himself falling through layers of the world's unheard agony.

And when he stopped screaming, he stopped falling. And when he opened his eyes he found himself bathed in the most splendid black starlight. And up above, like a forgotten god of the mountains, a towering colossus made of primal light, was the startling presence of the great archangel of invisibility.

One moment she was there; the next moment she was gone. Her presence was so brief that it seemed a lightning flash of eternity had passed through him. When the great archangel disappeared, leaving a glorious intensity of lights in the giant spaces she had occupied, with her wing span alone seeming to cover the entire island, he felt that he too had become completely insubstantial, and mightier. He was not sure how, or in what way.

'I don't understand anything at all,' he said to the wind.

'Don't try to understand,' the voice, his guide, said to him. 'Understanding comes beyond trying. It comes from beyond.'

'Beyond where?'

The voice stayed silent.

Six

He was still wondering about the places beyond, from which understanding comes, when he found himself at the foot of a fabulous bridge. The bridge, completely suspended in the air, held up by nothing that he could see, was a dazzling construct, composed entirely of mist. He was bewildered by the insubstantiality of the bridge. It too seemed to be made of light, of air, of feelings. He was afraid to step on it lest he would plunge down below.

'What holds up the bridge?' he asked his guide.

'Only the person crossing it,' came the reply.

'You mean that if I am to cross the bridge I must at the same time hold it up, keep it suspended?'

'Yes.'

'But how can I do both at the same time?'

'If you want to cross over you must. There is no other way.'

'And what lies below? I mean, if I should fail to hold it up while crossing what would I fall into? I ask because I do not see any water underneath.'

'There is no water underneath.'

'What is there underneath then?'

'Only those who fall know. And they have never returned to tell anyone else. We have our legend about what lies below, but the legend takes the form of a riddle which you must answer before you can be admitted into the palace.'

'So am I to make this crossing alone?'

'Yes.'

'And what about you?'

'I will be waiting for you on the other side.'

'But how will you get over without crossing?'

'That is something you can learn if you have crossed the bridge once. Not everyone learns it, of course. And many have forgotten; and because of that they have perished. On this island of ours learning what you know is something you have to do every day, and every moment.'

'In the places where I have been, forgetting is what you do every day.'

'Too much forgetting led to our great suffering. We always have to relearn here.'

'I have noticed also that I have grown heavier.'

'On our island heavier is lighter.'

'But if I am heavy will the bridge bear me?'

'If you can bear yourself, the bridge too can bear you.'

'And I must cross this bridge?'

'Yes, you must cross the bridge.'

'And if I do not cross?'

'You will be nowhere. In fact, you will be worse than nowhere. Everything around you will slowly disappear. Soon you will find yourself in an empty space. Then you will stiffen. You will lose all life. You will become the image of what you essentially are. Then, not long afterwards, half dead and half alive, unable to breathe and unable to die, you will become the statue of your worst and weakest self. In the morning, you will be collected by the garbage men and set up in the negative spaces of the city as another reminder to the inhabitants of the perils of failing to become what they can become. At night you will dream that you can move, and you will wander about in your own inferno, muttering strange words to those too idle to do anything else but listen. You will aid the island by becoming, at night, one of the negative dreams that test and tempt those who might receive prizes from the Academy of Integrity. I assure you, it is better to try to cross that bridge and fail, than to not try at all.'

Not long afterwards, he became aware that his guide had gone. The bridge was now invisible. He found himself looking into an unfathomable abyss.

Seven

He stood at the foot of the invisible bridge, with Time howling around him. He was filled with dread. He could see nothing beyond the abyss. He couldn't even see the other side of the bridge. He could no longer imagine his destination.

As he stood there, transfixed by the impossibility of going back or moving forward, he became aware that things were disappearing around him. An inscrutable mist seemed to be effacing the glass cupolas, the golden spires, the palace of mirrors, and the splendid marble facades of the island's incomparable streets. The mist seemed to be wiping out the divine forms which he had glimpsed in the moonlit air. As the mist effaced the colonnades and the marvellous ruins, the glowing hills and the chessboard universe, he realised to his horror that even the road behind him was becoming nothingness.

Time howled from the abyss as the creeping emptiness slowly enveloped the visible world. The emptiness began to devour even the sounds in the air and the mirages that his eyes had conjured in the mist.

'I did not come from nothing, and I will not die in nothing,' he said to himself.

But nothingness was blooming all about him in his unwillingness to cross the invisible bridge. Soon the empty spaces creeping towards him became a sort of white wind. The white wind blew away the foundations of the street, blew away the cypress trees, and even the gaps between things, upon which he had fixed his gaze, in the vain hope that while things disappeared the gaps between them would remain.

'I will not die in nothing,' he said again, as he watched the world slide away from him into an avalanche of invisibility.

Soon he felt himself standing on the last remaining patch of earth in the whole world. Soon he felt himself on the last ledge of a precipice. Soon he felt his senses falling under the beautiful seduction of the abyss. Out of its enigma he heard soft susurrations and gentle whispers, as of voices murmuring consolations to the last man on earth, who thought himself damned. But when he listened more attentively he thought he could distinguish low songs, sweet tender choruses of the abyss calling him into the happy home of the world-effacing white wind.

For a moment, he was blissful. For a moment, he was seduced. The abyss seemed the perfect place to rest, the safest harbour from so much anxious questing after visibility. It seemed the true home he had been seeking all his life. Slowly, in his mind first, be began to succumb to sleep. Slowly, in his body next, he felt himself falling. There was a grace and a loveliness in his dream of falling. Then, just before he succumbed completely to the song of the abyss, it occurred to him that the nothingness that was devouring the visible world was now beginning to devour him.

In the space of a moment, he felt himself turning to stone. In the space of another moment, he saw himself as a negative statue, with a vacuous happiness on his face. The vision filled him with horror.

'No, I was not born into nothing,' he cried to himself, as he made one last effort to rally his mind.

And when he looked about him with eyes already heavy-lidded with the sweetness of falling, what he saw made him cry out with infernal dread. Years later, he would remember that terror also has its enchantment and its uses. It was the terror of what he saw that probably woke him up to the last moment of his old life.

Eight

All around emptiness bristled like a snow-drift. The white winds whipped the last spaces on the highest mountain and all he could see below was the pure whiteness of oblivion. The universe had collapsed on itself and he stood on a tiny patch of earth that had turned white like a frosted mirror. And in his ears, he heard the happy wailings of the devouring wind. He was becoming nothing. He was dissolving into negative space. And he felt it was worse than dying. At least with dying he would be falling away from the world into an unknown. Now he was falling from nothingness into something more horrible than nothing.

Even the moon had gone. The absence of the archangel had left him in the loneliest place in the world. There was now nothing behind him, and a bridge of dreams before him. He felt that he was living the meaning of his life for the first time.

In the space of that defining moment, he noticed that the bridge had suddenly become visible. He was about to move when the bridge became invisible again, tantalising him.

The wind had begun effacing the frosted mirror beneath his feet when the bridge appeared again, but in the form of water. Then it turned into a bridge of stone. Then it turned into a bridge of fire. And he knew instinctively, as the white wind began to efface him out of existence, that if the bridge turned from fire into anything else he would be doomed forever in nothingness.

Screaming as he had screamed when he fell into the abyss of invisibility, he ran onto the bridge of fire.

Nine

He half expected to fall through the flames. In his panic he had forgotten his fear that the bridge might not be real. He fled across the bridge and slowly became aware that the faster he ran the less distance he covered and the hotter the flames were. It occurred to him to slow down. He proceeded to walk. His panic changed. The heat from the fiery bridge lessened. He gained some confidence from the curious fact that the fire seemed to bear his weight.

Then he noticed that the slower he walked through the flames of the bridge, the greater the distance he seemed to cover, and the faster he seemed to move. He was beginning to enjoy these strange little discoveries when he remembered that the flames were supposed to burn him. In that moment, almost as if he had created it with his fear, he felt the unbearable heat from the railings and girders of fire. He felt himself burning. He felt his feet and his back and his hair and his face sizzling in the midst of the red and blue tongues of fire. He turned and started to run back in a new panic when suddenly the dancing yellow flames raced down from his hair and began to consume his flesh.

Howling, he threw himself on the floor of the roaring furnace all around, screaming into his own maddened agony. Burning all over, feeling himself turning cinderous, he jumped back up and was about to leap off the bridge into what he hoped was the perfectly cooling water of the abyss when something changed all about him.

Suddenly, he felt himself flailing and kicking, turning and sinking into the liquid floor of the furnace.

Confused, thrashing about, he found himself beginning to drown.

Halfway across, the bridge had turned into water.

Ten

Bewildered by the sudden flooding of the bridge, he started to swim. He swam in a panic, forgetting what his guide had told him – that every moment he had to relearn what he already knew. And so the faster he swam, the slower he moved, till it appeared as if all his confused efforts only succeeded in making him go backwards. He resisted this paradox of motion with all his might and all his fear, and soon found himself near the beginning of the bridge again.

It was only then that he remembered the mysterious quality of grace that his guide had hinted at. And he remembered only because he didn't want to have to go through it all over again, making all the mistakes of his confusion. So he swam more gently, more slowly, and he wasn't at all surprised that this made him travel faster through the water.

He was beginning to enjoy the serenity in this discovery when it occurred to him that he was swimming in the air, in an illusion, in a dream, and that at any moment he would fall through the water into the dreaded abyss below.

He had barely completed this thought when he found himself in midair, with voices crying around him, with demons rushing past his face, whistling songs from his childhood. He noticed strange beings with green eyes, riding on yellow horses, drifting past his gaze. He was surprised to find people wandering past him in the air, dressed in blues and reds, with a distracted look in their eyes.

As if in a mist, he saw whole peoples rising from the depths of a great ocean, rising from the forgetful waters. Then, with a fixed and mystic gaze in their eyes, he saw them walking to an island of dreams. There they began building a great city of stone, and within it mighty pyramids and universities and churches and libraries and palaces and all the new unseen wonders of the world. He saw them building a great new future in an invisible space. They built quietly for a thousand years. They built a new world of beauty and wisdom and protection and joy to compensate for their five hundred years of suffering and oblivion beneath the ocean. They had dwelt as forgotten skeletons on the ocean bed, among the volcanic stones and the dead creatures that turn into diamonds, among the fishes of wonder that never come to the surface to bathe in sunlight. He noticed that there is also light in the depths.

He saw all these things as he flailed in midspace.

Then he realised that towards the end, the bridge had turned into air, and into dreams.

Eleven

He marvelled at the dreams, and at how clear they were. He marvelled at the people who had risen, as if from a millennial sleep, from the ocean bed that had been their home. And he was filled with wonder at the great and enduring beauty of the new civilisation they had built for themselves in their invisible spaces. They had built it as their sanctuary. It was the fruit of what they had learned during those long years of suffering and oblivion at the bottom of the ocean. They had built a fabulous civilisation of stone and marble, of diamond and gold. They had constructed palaces of wisdom, libraries of the infinite, cathedrals of joy, courts of divine laws, streets of bliss, cupolas of nobility, pyramids of light. They had fashioned a civic society in which the highest possibilities of the inhabitants could be realised. They had invented mystery schools and rituals of illumination. They had created an educational system in which the most ordinary goal was living the fullest life, in which creativity in all spheres of endeavour was the basic alphabet, and in which the most sublime lessons possible were always learned and relearned from the unforgettable suffering which was the bedrock of their great new civilisation.

He was stunned by the beauty of their eternal sculptings. Their paintings were glorious: they seemed to have reached such heights of development that the works imparted the psychic luminosity of their artistry in mysterious colours, concealed forms, and even more concealed subjects.

Awed by their majestic festivals, astonished by the infinite ways in which everything done in the civilisation was touched with wisdom, and inspiring of passionate delight, he found himself soaring in the dreams of this mysterious people.

He had never been so happy as he was in the great dreams. His joy was so intense that he became aware of himself in the air, invisible, a pure vibration of bliss, a bird of light. And he wondered how long he would exist in this beatification before he would find himself falling back towards the stones of a familiar reality.

He had hardly completed this thought, floating above the dreams of the cultivated hills of serenity, when he felt himself falling. He was falling through the air, with the beautiful visions drifting away from him. And his fall was so strange that when he found himself on solid ground, standing there as if he had never made a single motion all his life, he was completely surprised.

He did not have to look to know that the bridge had become solid again.

Twelve

When he did look back, however, he found himself at the end of the most magnificent bridge he would ever see. He thought of it as the bridge of self-discovery. It was a great marble bridge with gold incrustations and diamond girders. Sweeping over the air in a majestic curve, it seemed to be made of a substance that created its own light. Its light irradiated the seven hills.

He was still marvelling at the bridge and at the curious nature of his crossing, when he became aware of the silent presence of his guide.

'I don't think I will ever understand,' he said.

'Understanding often leads to ignorance, especially when it comes too soon,' replied his guide.

'But if I don't understand how can I carry on?'

'It's because you don't understand that you carry on.'

'But I have to make sense of what I have just experienced.'

'When you make sense of something, it tends to disappear. It is only mystery which keeps things alive,' said his guide, patiently.

It was the patience in his guide's voice that made him look back. When he looked back, he was astonished to find that the bridge had disappeared. It occurred to him that he had somehow managed to walk across emptiness. For the first time, touched with a magical humility, he realised the nature of the small miracle he had enacted in his life.

Making no allusion to his crossing of the abyss, his guide led him into the city of the Invisibles.

BOOK TWO

One

They went down stone streets, with silence echoing about them. The city was empty, but he felt presences everywhere. He couldn't explain it, but it seemed the air was watching him.

In the darkness the buildings loomed like materialised dreams. They seemed like great constructs on a giant stage set. He felt small amongst the mighty stone edifices.

They went into the city at the most mysterious time of night, when footsteps were heard and no one was seen, or when a song would drift past in the air, disembodied.

His guide was silent. But at the darkest hour he seemed to notice a golden glow beside him as they passed the open spaces with marble fountains and elegant stone monoliths where the founding fathers of legend had made the public declaration of the creation of a new civilisation.

The glow that was his guide was intense in the open legendary spaces. The marble fountains, seven in all, had the sculptings of rare ocean-bed fishes with brilliantly lit water spouting from their mouths. On the stone monoliths had been inscribed the original words of the initiators of the new civilisation — words that had the brevity and authority of universal laws. They were words of a language that he couldn't decode, a language no longer spoken. Then he realised that all along he had assumed a similarity of language, when in fact he had been communicating with his guide beyond words.

They crossed the shining open spaces and came to an array of streets. The houses, buildings, and offices were all majestic, and all of stone, but it was of a stone that seemed in a permanent state of dreaming.

As he passed them he felt that one day he would understand their dreams.

Two

The air was full of harmonies. He breathed them in. Elated with the harmonies in the air, he was surprised to find that it wasn't the buildings with their clarity of construction, their musical forms, their chaste pillars, and their ancient moods that so affected him. There was no denying the nobility of the tenements and the purity of the abodes: they made the spaces into something dream-like. But what affected him the most, as he went down the narrow streets, were the myths and the magic in the air.

All things invisible had a hidden glow to them. He sensed in that world something higher than marble and gold. He sensed a spirit of hidden light everywhere, concealed behind the mighty churches and the great basilicas of justice.

The myths in the air made him feel as if he had left his body and entered a temple of world dreams. This was compounded by melodies heard and not located. It occurred to him that the city was composed of songs, and that the stones were singing. It occurred to him that the marble facades and the radiant statues, the stained-glass cathedrals and the merchant banks, the emporiums and the visible buildings of state, the yellow order of it all and violet perfection of the streets had been erected, put in place, and shaped purely by music, and by spirit.

It was the harmonies in the air that made him sense that the visible city was a pretext and a guise for an invisible realm. All things suggested something divine.

As he passed the silent mausoleums and the celebratory arches and the temples touched with the blue light of that darkness, he sensed that the visible city was a dream meant to deceive the eyes of men. He sensed that everything seen was intended to be visible only that it should pass away.

The hidden harmonies in the air seemed to mock the grandeur that he saw in the golden cupolas, the oriel windows, and the sprawling palaces.

Then, as he contemplated this hint of the destructibility of all things seen, he became aware that what first seemed like a city of stone was really a city of water. It appeared briefly to be a realm beneath the deepest ocean, where the purest sunlight pours out from below, where memory no longer reaches, and where living eyes have never been.

Three

He was about to ask a question of his guide when he felt from the harmonies in the air a modest injunction to silence. The glow that was his guide floated serenely beside him, illuminating the way.

He walked on in the silver melodies. He breathed in fragrances of tenderness, and breathed out his anxieties. He swam in his questions. He had never felt so weightless.

The city was a world; and the world was telling him things that he couldn't understand for many years to come.

As he walked though, listening to his happy footfalls, he felt the world was telling him to stop looking, for then he would see beyond; to stop thinking, for then he would comprehend; to stop trying to make sense of things, for then he would find the truest grace.

Four

Then, quite imperceptibly, things began to change. The roof-tops, which at first seemed uniform under the blue light of darkness, became more distinct. And yet, all about him, the city was yielding its forms. Houses seemed to turn into liquid, and to flow away before he reached them. A horse in the distance became a mist when he got there. Fountains dissolved into fragrances. Palaces became empty spaces where trees dwelt in solitude. Cathedrals became vacant places where harmonies were sweetest in the air.

It suddenly appeared odd to him, but the solid things of the city seemed like ideas. And ideas, which were alive in the air, seemed to him like solid things. A house of justice became a mood of green. The fragrance of roses turned into the statues of five Africans along the street. A melody which he started to hum became a giant sun-dial. And a happy mood which seized him turned into the great tombs of the earliest mothers of that land.

Five

'What manner of place is this', he asked eventually, 'where nothing is what it seems?'

'Everything is what it seems,' replied his guide. 'It's only you who are not what you seem.'

'What am I then that I am not what I seem?'

'That is for you to say.'

'I think I am what I seem.'

'What are you then?'

'An ordinary man in a strange place.'

'Might you not be a strange man in an ordinary place?'

'How can you call this place ordinary?' he cried to his guide. 'Everything keeps becoming something else. I thought I saw a horse back there, but when I neared it the horse turned into mist.'

'You saw the horse in the mist. You did the seeing.'

'But everything seems to whisper.'

'You hear the whispers.'

'The air is full of sounds.'

'The air is always full of sounds.'

'Even the silences have melodies.'

'Silence is a sort of melody.'

'And where is everyone? Is this an empty city, are there no inhabitants?'

'The city sleeps. The inhabitants dream.'

'So you mean that this is an ordinary city?'

'As it should be.'

'And there is nothing odd about it?'

'Only the oddness that the few visitors bring, or that the inhabitants choose to feel.'

He was silent. It amazed him, for a moment, to think that he could hear his guide smiling.

Six

He had been walking for a while, listening to the smile of his guide, when it occurred to him that he was entering the city for the second time. He seemed to have come back to the place just after the bridge. He became aware of it because of a mood of orange jubilation that passed above him. When he looked up he saw himself under a celebratory arch. He had passed that place before but hadn't been aware of it. He had only been aware of the mood.

To his consternation, he found himself walking into the city again. He went down its narrow streets, past its stained-glass houses, and past the mist which turned into a horse.

When he looked back and saw the horse turning into fire, he screamed.

His guide smiled. He felt the smile as a radiance of warm light, a gentle blaze.

The melodies in the air became something that either cooled or heated his body. Some melodies almost made him quiver.

Houses that he had passed, with their inspired rustications and their perfect caryatids, burst into splendid flames when he looked back at them. The air was full of fire. The street began to burn. The fountains spouted golden flames. Marigold fires erupted from the churches. And the house of justice was a blue furnace, burning with cool intensity into the unaltered night.

The golden cupolas were majestic balls of rotating fire. The palaces all over the hills were a dance of flames, burning in rainbow colours. And the spires, pointing like golden-blue swords of incandescence towards the cool constellations, shimmered in the city air.

Everything was so touched and possessed by this almost divine fire that for a long moment he could not breathe.

The jade dragon projecting from the entablature of a bank seemed to roar with a tender blaze. The banks were aglow with silver and yellow. The streets, like a flaming ultramarine river, flowed underneath him. And yet he was not consumed. Instead, he was possessed with a happy mood, a mood of joyful fervour, of sublime terror.

At first he had seen the place as a city of stone, then as one of water. Now he knew it to be a city of the purest fire.

Seven

It was only after a while that he realised that the pure fire of the city was burning parts of him away, burning away something within him. He breathed in the fire, and began to see things differently.

He saw an illuminated world, a world that was a living painting. In the animated painting he saw blue houses, yellow trees, black flowers, golden farmers in their diamond fields, a blue and yellow and red earth, yellow riders on blue and yellow horses, aquamarine birds, and an emerald dawn.

The world was aflame with colour. The world was drunk on colour. He became quite colour-mad.

The street was now of burnt sienna. The statues were of vermilion hue. The fountains spouted twinkling water that seemed to smile. The stars were green. The earth became topaz. And the air was oceanic blue.

He breathed in the colours, amazed at the cities hidden within the city.

Eight

And as he breathed in deeply the changing colours of the air, he noticed that the glow that was his guide seemed to be floating.

'What is the first law of this place?' he asked his floating guide.

'The first law of our city', the guide said, with that almost ironic smile in the voice, 'is that what you think is what becomes real.'

He pondered this as he walked past fountains and alongside the fields of dancing colours that he had already passed before.

'Does that mean if I think I have passed the same place twice it too becomes real?'

'Yes.'

'But what if I pass it twice before I think it?'

'That means you were not aware of it the first time. Anything you are not aware of you have to experience again.'

'Why?'

'Because if you weren't aware of it, you didn't pass it. You didn't experience it.'

'But what if I am aware of the second time?'

'Then you experienced it once. The law is simple. Every experience is repeated or suffered till you experience it properly and fully the first time.'

'Why is this so?'

'It is one of the foundations of our civilisation. At the beginning of our history there was great suffering. Our sages learnt that we tend to repeat our suffering if we have not learnt fully all that can be learnt from it. And so we had to experience our suffering completely while it happened so it would be so deeply lodged in our memory and in our desire for a higher life that we would never want to experience the suffering again, in any form. Hence the law. Anyone who sleeps through their experiences would have to undergo them for as many times as it takes to wake them up and make them feel the uniqueness or the horror of their experiences for the first time. This law is the basis of our civilisation, a permanent sense of wonder at the stillness of time.'

'Is time still?'

'Does time move?'

'Yes.'

'Where to?'

'I don't know.'

'Have you seen it move?'

'Yes.'

'Where?'

'On a sundial.'

'That is the measurement of a motion. Time itself is invisible. It is not a river. While you are in time all time is still. As in a painting.'

'But day turns into night.'

'Yes.'

'So time moves.'

'No. The planet moves. Time is still.'

'I don't understand.'

'That's because you move your mind too much.'
'What then is the second law of this place?'
'When you need to know it you will find out.'
'You are a difficult guide.'
'Wait till you meet the others.'
With this remark, his guide fell silent again.

Nine

He had been walking, had been listening to his guide, been listening to the colours in the air, but he hadn't been paying much attention to the world about him. He hadn't noticed that scenes he was passing were ones he had already passed without being aware of the repetition. The journey seemed endless.

He saw the apple-green towers, and he noticed the horse as a white mist on a floating cloud of stone. He felt himself to be weightless again. He looked about him in shock, as if he had been rudely woken from sleep, from a dream in a painting. The spires were bright red, quivering beneath the dancing silver specks of the stars. The great dome, now barely visible amongst the clouds, was a revolving whorl of yellow and rose. The street was floating. The whole city seemed to be a great island on a cloud. The distant hills were adrift. The stained-glass cathedral was a song of glinting emerald. He saw that the city was in the air, and he felt dizzy.

It occurred to him for the first time that he wasn't walking into the city but that he was walking through realms, through dimensions.

His guide said:

'When you stop inventing reality then you see things as they really are.'

He said:

'But I can't seem to stop.'

His guide said:

'There is a time for inventing reality, and there is a time for being still. At the gate of every new reality you must be still, or you won't be able to enter properly.'

'How do I learn to be still?'

'No one can teach you such things. You have to learn for yourself.'

Ten

His guide paused. Then, as if conscious of the wasted generosity of what he was about to impart, but having faith anyway, the guide said:

'Do you realise that you know more than you think you know? Do you realise that if you use all you know, and all the possibilities within you, that there is almost nothing that you can't do? More serious than that is this fact: if you use more than you know that you know, the world will be as paradise. What we know compared to what we don't know is like a grain of sand compared to a mountain. But what we don't know, our unsuspected possibilities, is immense in us. That is our true power and kingdom. When nations do amazing things, that is because they create from what they know. And that is a lot. When they do extraordinary things, that is because they create from places in themselves they didn't suspect were there. But when a nation or an individual creates things so sublime – in a sort of permanent genius of inventiveness and delight – when they create things so miraculous that they are not seen or noticed or remarked upon by even the best minds around, then that is because they create always from the vast unknown places within them. They create always from beyond. They make the undiscovered places and infinities in them their friend. They live on the invisible fields of their hidden genius.

And so their most ordinary achievements are always touched with genius. Their most ordinary achievements, however, are what the world sees, and acclaims. But their most extra-ordinary achievements are unseen, invisible, and therefore cannot be destroyed. This endures forever. Such is the dream and reality of this land. I speak with humility.'

Eleven

His guide laughed for the last time. It was a prelude to a long silence. But before that he said:

'All that you will see are the lesser things, the things meant to perish. The most important things are the things you don't see. The best things here are in the invisible realm. It has taken us much suffering, much repetition of our suffering, much stupidity, many mistakes, great patience, and phenomenal love to arrive at this condition. However, changes are coming. You are the herald of changes. We have not had a visible being here for a very long time. The changes may be terrible, and would seem to be catastrophic. But it has all been foretold. The changes, however, would be an illusion, an excuse for the invisible powers to continue on higher and hidden levels. Without these changes we tend to forget.'

The guide stopped suddenly. Then, just as suddenly, he continued.

'And so, as you are about to enter our realm, and as I might not see you again, let me tell you two things. The first is that a great law guides the rise and fall of things. What is of the greatest importance grows and keeps on growing as a result of this. Don't despair too much if you see beautiful things destroyed, if you see them perish. Because the best things are always growing in secret. We have discovered an invisible way.

The next stage of our evolution is to be free of our visible things. Then we will become sublime forces in the universe. Therefore, don't despair if you see death. Nothing really dies. The unseen things are our masterpieces. The seen things are merely byproducts. What would seem like victory would be a defeat. What would seem like defeat would be a victory, an eternal victory of Light.'

Twelve

He was overwhelmed by what his guide had revealed to him.

'You have told me many things,' he said, humbly.

His guide replied:

'No, I have told you less than one thing. Forget what I say, then maybe you will remember. But you will remember in spirit.'

The guide paused, then said:

'The second thing I have to say to you is this.'

And the guide, filling the spaces with the warm brilliant glow of an invisible smile, seemed to take a deep breath as if for a great speech. But he stayed silent. The silence changed the colours all around. The silence seemed to go on forever, in wave after wave.

After a while, spinning in this silence, he became aware that the glow that was his guide was no longer there. The space about him was devoid of that intense and ultramarine personality, that presence of gold. His guide did not speak again. His guide was gone.

BOOK THREE

BOOK THREE

One

He was alone. He had seldom felt so alone. And when he had recovered sufficiently from his surprise at his guide's silent departure, he found that he was standing before the great gate of the city.

He must have passed through the gate several times already, but he was only aware of it now for the first time. It was such an imposing gate, rising high into the clouds, fashioned of gold and diamond and flashing steel. It was a gate so mighty that it seemed designed for colossal beings. He wondered how he'd had the nerve to pass through it several times without noticing.

Now that he was aware of the gate, he found himself unable to move. Surmounted by a giant dragon with fiery eyes and metal claws and fantastic wings as wide as the rooftop of a house, the gate was truly terrifying. But the terror of the gate was also beautiful. Its beauty made the terror worse.

Along the grilles, the metal bands and on the niches were figures wrought in red gold, figures of ancient heroes, of monsters, heads bristling with a network of spikes and snakes. All the figures stared at him menacingly.

The gate seemed so alive with intent that he wasn't sure what to do. He felt that he had no right to pass through. He felt that he needed permission. And yet the gate was wide open, and there was no one in sight.

Two

As he studied the harmonic monstrosity of the gate, he became conscious of an iron scroll high up in the air, clasped in one of the paws of the winged dragon. The metal scroll had embossed figures of a shark, a dolphin, a lion, an eagle, the sphinx, the phoenix, the eagle, and the griffin. It also had strange deep-water creatures with seven eyes.

At the top of the scroll was the bronze sculpting of a lamp. The lamp shone in the darkness, spreading light and yet creating no shadows.

On the scroll itself were words inscribed in a language he couldn't decipher, the motto of the gate. He tried hard to read the words, to understand their prescription, but the longer he looked at the words the more things seemed to dissolve and change around him till he felt sure that the gate itself was a living thing, a monster in iron. More than that, he felt certain that the gate was moving, that it was bearing down on him.

Three

He couldn't move. Magnetised by the words, he was also unable to think. The gargoyles and the lapis lazuli snakes seemed to writhe and hiss. The giant dragon seemed to breathe out an invisible devouring fire. Its fabulous wings appeared to stir.

Then, to his horror, the open spaces of the gate, through which he should pass, began to howl.

The wind bristled with enigmas and hints, with warnings whispered round his head. A strange heat blasted his eyes.

The open spaces of the gate were more terrifying than the gate itself. And more terrifying than the space were the undeciphered words.

He knew that if he couldn't decipher the words he would never be able to enter the city. He knew he would earn the right to pass into that strange domain only if he could also solve the riddle of the gate. And he knew that, like the bridge and the crossing of the abyss, the longer it took him the greater was his peril. Only this time he had no guide to explain to him the full nature of his impending doom.

Four

He had been standing before the gate, in a condition of mounting fear, when he realised that just above his gaze was an equestrian figure bearing aloft a mighty axe. The axe was poised right above his head. It occurred to him to move backwards, or step sideways, but he couldn't.

His panic grew worse. He started to quiver. He felt something strange all around him; he felt presences and vague forms encompassing him, pressing down on him in the darkness. Unable to master his incomprehension, unable to breathe, unable to think, he started to tremble. It seemed that the whole world was trembling with him.

A grey mist covered his eyes. His whole being was atremble now with an uncontrollable horror at once beautiful and humbling. He was all dissolved within. He felt like a child abandoned on the highest peak of a mountain, or on the edge of an endless sea, or in a deep night with no illumination anywhere in the universe. Tears poured down his face and he wept like a child, trembling without knowing why, and quivering under the mystery of the wind blowing through the negative spaces of the great gate.

Five

The more he trembled, the purer the lamp shone, and the clearer the words became. It was as if the words were a law he had known all his life, a pitiless law which when forgotten creates its own punishment. And the punishment was that of complete abandonment, till the condition of the words was reached. Then it would be no longer necessary to know what the words were, because the person waiting at the gate would have become the words, would have incarnated them.

He was becoming the words as he trembled in his emptiness. A moment before he felt certain that the horseman's axe was going to split his skull in two, a moment before the dreadful empty space completely invaded his mind, and before the vague forms pounced on him in their numinous threat, he felt himself falling. But this time, he fell to the ground. He jumped back up as soon as he touched the cold marble of the road.

When he looked about him, he was astonished to find that the gate had vanished. In its place was a voice. It was the voice of a child, a little boy. And the boy, with a strange coldness, said:

'I am your new guide. I am sent to lead you to the square.'

The boy too was invisible. Still possessed by the spirit of trembling, in a state of complete humility and gratitude, he followed his new guide through the mysterious gate of the city.

Six

He saw the city now as he had never seen it before. He didn't see the things of the city; he saw the things that weren't there. It was the trembling that caused this new sensitivity. He saw how alive the invisible spaces were. He saw the light concealed in the darkness. And he heard the silence. It was cool on his ears. He went into the city, treading carefully, alive to the spaces, aware of everything, aware as only the very scared or the very humble can be. His new guide was silent, and explained nothing.

He walked through the city of sensitive stone, and even the silence of his child-guide helped him to understand that the city was also aware of him. The city was listening. He could hear its attentiveness.

The streets shone in the dark. He sensed that though the streets were made of marble they were paved with the beauty that only the wisest people can create from suffering. The suffering was there in the beauty of everything. It was there in the infinite care of the city's planning, in its clarity.

Everywhere the city's nominal origins were visible. Many houses were shaped like coral reefs. Many buildings seemed to be made into something fluid. And there were underwater plants over the houses. Fountains spouted water at regular intervals. It was a city of stone and fire, but its true inspiration was water.

The buildings were both hard and gentle. Even the defensive parapets and the strategic battlements were meant to deceive. He felt that the solid facades, the strong lines, the massive abodes, the square-shaped clusters of rooftops, imposing on the outside, hid tenderness and gardens on the inside.

It was a place that understood that the good things should be visible, but the best things should be hidden.

Seven

Suddenly, he saw the city as a vast network of thoughts. Courts were places where people went to study the laws, not places of judgement. The library, which he took to be one building, but which he later discovered was practically the whole city, was a place where people went to record their thoughts, their dreams, their intuitions, their ideas, their memories, and their prophecies. They also went there to increase the wisdom of the race. Books were not borrowed. Books were composed there, and deposited.

The universities were places for self-perfection, places for the highest education in life. Everyone taught everyone else. All were teachers, all were students. The sages listened more than they talked; and when they talked it was to ask questions that would engage endless generations in profound and perpetual discovery.

The universities and the academies were also places where people sat and meditated and absorbed knowledge from the silence. Research was a permanent activity, and all were researchers and appliers of the fruits of research. The purpose was to discover the hidden unifying laws of all things, to deepen the spirit, to make more profound the sensitivities of the individual to the universe, and to become more creative.

Love was the most important subject in the universities.

Entire faculties were devoted to the art of living. The civilisation was dedicated to a simple goal, the perfection of the spirit and the mastery of life.

Eight

A fragrance of eternity lingered over everything, like the aroma of flowers in spring. The fragrance didn't come from the buildings, the churches, the ordered streets, the ochre skyline of rooftops, or from the concealed gardens. The fragrance was a part of the spaces: it was as if the city was continuously freshened by breezes from the arbours of a hidden god.

Nine

He was surprised to know, in a flash, without being told, that banks were places where people deposited or withdrew thoughts of well-being, thoughts of wealth, thoughts of serenity. When people were ill they went to their banks. When healthy, they went to the hospitals.

The hospitals were places of laughter, amusement, and recreation. They were houses of joy. The doctors and nurses were masters of the art of humour, and they all had to be artists of one kind or another.

It was a unique feature of the place, but the hospitals had their facades painted by the great masters of art. They were some of the most beautiful and harmonious buildings in the city. Merely looking at them lifted the spirits.

The masters of the land believed that sickness should be cured before it became sickness. The healthy were therefore presumed sick. Healing was always needed, and was considered a necessary part of daily life. Healing was always accompanied by the gentlest music. When healing was required the sick ones lingered in the presence of great paintings, and sat in wards where masterpieces of healing composition played just below the level of hearing. Outdoor activity, sculpting, story-telling, poetry, and laughter were the most preferred forms of treatment. Contemplation of the sea and of the people's origins and of their destiny was considered the greatest cure for sickness before it became sickness.

The inhabitants of that land, who were the hardest workers in the universe, were seldom ill. When they were ill at all, it was in order to regenerate their dreams and visions.

They went to the hospitals to improve their art of breathing. They went for stillness. They went there to remember their beginnings and to keep in mind their ever-elusive destination. Hospitals were places where the laws of the universe were applied. Individuals, mostly, healed themselves. The art of self-healing was the fourth most important aspect of their education.

Ten

He understood all this in flashes as he passed the incomprehensible buildings and read the indecipherable signs. He began to suspect that somehow, without trying, he understood more than he was aware. And through all this his child-guide remained silent.

He passed shops, where people exchanged the fruits of their talents, rather than sold goods for money. The concept of money was alien to the city. The only form of money it had consisted in the quality of thoughts, ideas, and possibilities. With a fine idea a house could be purchased. With a brilliant thought rooftops could be restored. Useful new ways of seeing things, imparted possibilities, could be exchanged for acres of land. The currencies of the civilisation were invisible, and had to do with values. There was no hunger in the city. The only hunger there was existed in the city's dream for a sublime future.

As he noticed and sensed these things he wondered about the kind of suffering that inspired this unending quest for the highest, this loving vigilance, this near-perfection of justice. It seemed to him that it must be a suffering which keeps renewing itself in the soul, which refuses to be forgotten, a suffering which demands to be continually turned into gold.

The thought somehow frightened him. He knew that the

inhabitants were not inhuman. He knew that they had perfected the art of invisibility, and could not be seen by him. But he began to wonder if they were gods, or if as a people they were becoming almost divine, through careful spiritual and social evolution. The possibility of a whole people approaching, in their humanity, the condition of divinity, scared and astonished him. The thought that suffering could give people insights into the intersection of life and eternity filled him with amazement.

Eleven

Stopping to breathe a moment, he tried to recover from the wonderful notions with which the city assaulted him.

He came to the piazza of festivities. Even at night he could hear all the celebrations of the distant ages that the stones and fountains and silent buildings gave out in their dreaming. He wandered through the piazza's memories of pageants and histories and festivals. The piazza, in its silence, seemed always to be in a carnival mood, seemed always to be laughing.

In the city everything remembers, and freely yields its memories like certain flowers in moonlight.

Twelve

A delighted mood blossomed in him as he passed the glittering arcades and marketplaces where the Invisibles from all over the world came to buy and sell ideas. Here they traded in philosophies, inspirations, intuitions, prophecies, paradoxes, riddles, enigmas, visions, and dreams. Enigmas were their trinkets, philosophies their jewelleries, paradoxes their silver, clarity their measure, inspiration their gold, prophecy their language, vision their play, and dreams their standard.

The season's fashion was for paradoxes, and the marketplace, even at night, was abuzz with fresh-minted paradoxes and ancient riddles from the farthest corners of the world. The air was scented with them. Enigmas twinkled over the arcade roofs, with shining eyes, like owls at play. Paradoxes flew about in the emporiums, like birds of joy. Riddles danced in the dark places, like blissful fireflies. Beautiful lights thrilled in his spirit. He quivered in a sparkling sense of a renewed childhood. For the first time since his arrival, he smiled.

Thirteen

He had passed the marts and the marketplaces of ideas, and was still smiling, when he saw an elongated glow in the distance moving towards him. Because of the glow he noticed the peculiarly ancient and velvet quality of the night.

The air was very warm and it smelt of old stones. It smelt also of marble, of the serenity that comes after centuries of turbulence, and curiously, also, of fragrant earth. He sensed that a divine mother ruled the night of the city. Her warm presence was both protective and enduring.

He seemed to float through the warm air. Thrilling to the melody of enigmas, he was nonetheless troubled by the approaching glow. It was like an omen. As the glow in the distance came closer he was able to distinguish four shining lamps in the air, moving without support, borne aloft and floating along with a stately majesty. There was something ceremonial about the way the lamps glided through the air, shedding a bright light which cast no shadows.

Then he heard the solemn music of the lute. The quiet tones dispelled the darkness with their ritual sounds. The music was sad and funereal. As he listened a tragic mood came over him, followed by a plaintive breeze which made him quiver. It was as if he had sensed the symmetry of fate.

The elongated glow became a litter. Lying flat on the

decorated litter, as if dead, was a woman dressed in white and gold. Her horizontal form dazzled in the night. It dazzled with sequins and sparkling jewellery. A resplendent triangle of light hung just above her head. Wrapped around her, as if made from the breeze, was a muslin cloth. She had flowers round her flowing hair, flowers between her breasts, and about her legs. She was very beautiful, like a lost angel, and a great unhappiness made her beauty shine. An amazing light shone all about her. She looked like a princess being borne off to her nocturnal bridegroom, or to her gilded resting place among the fragrant marble of a royal tomb.

He heard light funereal singing in front of her, accompanying the paradoxically joyful lutes. She was on the litter, floating in the air, with nothing bearing her aloft, except the night and the fateful breeze. The sweetly mournful music changed the air around and resounded gently off the listening stones and the ancient houses.

Filled with curiosity, he broke off from his invisible guide and followed the floating litter. He stared with fascination at the first visible being he had seen since his disembarkation.

As he stared with wide-eyed amazement, the woman suddenly opened her eyes. When she saw him she screamed piercingly into the night. The footfalls around her hurried on, and she glided more speedily through the air. The music sped on too. And the singing remained faithful to its solemnity.

He ran after her. She was sitting up now on the litter of gold brocade and rich green velvet. Flowers poured down her face like tears. She stared at him with terror and sadness in her eyes. When he got close enough to her he said:

'Where are they taking you?'

She seemed surprised that he had spoken. He asked the

question again. This time she heard him clearly, and a sigh escaped her lips. Then with a sad voice, she cried:

'I am going where I can see people, and where people can see me.'

'What do you mean?'

'I am going where there is some illusion,' she cried again.

He was puzzled.

'Too much beauty is bad for the soul,' she said. 'I want illusion. I want some ugliness. I want some suffering. I want to be visible.'

'But I can see you,' he shouted.

'That's because I'm leaving. Besides, you are the only one who can.'

'Why?'

'You are doomed.'

'How?'

'Doomed, or a bringer of doom.'

He stopped running after her. He was a little out of breath. He was also bewildered.

'I hope I never meet your type again,' she screamed, as if distracted.

'I want to be visible!' she wailed. 'I want to be seen!'

He watched the litter grow smaller. His guide, in a cool voice, said:

'Do you want to carry on to the square, or do you want to follow her?'

He watched as the litter stopped in front of a huge set of marble columns. Then, with mounting apprehension, he watched as it disappeared into the splendid facade of a granite temple.

Her wailing had ceased. The music was gentler. And the

singing became more beautiful as it grew fainter.

Just before she vanished into the temple, he thought he saw her smile. It occurred to him that maybe she too was a paradox. Unaccountably, he sensed that somewhere in the future, in another realm, he would see her again.

Conscious for the first time that his guide had been communing with him all along, and feeling the awesome mystery of the night stealing into his bones, he continued with his journey towards the square.

Fourteen

He soared with an inexplicable joy when he got to the square. The tender air and the ancient palace, rectilinear and dream-like, seemed to have drifted in from the happy realms of a forgotten childhood. He couldn't understand what it was about the square that made him feel as if he had come home after years of wandering.

The palace dominating the square was of ochred stone, and it rose high up into the maternal darkness. It was so huge that it seemed to be part of the night, and seemed to belong to the substance of all dreams. And yet it was like a spectacular stage set, lit up with coloured flares. Banners and bunting and a night-coloured flag fluttered in the breeze from its highest battlements. Pennants shone below. The palace gate was of the finest and oldest bronze. And on the gate had been carved the most extraordinary shapes of gods, and angels, and sleeping women.

Fifteen

The hidden spaces in the square were vast and full of gentle presences. The open air seemed eternal, as if the wind blew in from great seas. And yet there were buildings all about, partially blocking off the corners of the square. He glimpsed the passageways and the secret streets.

Opposite the mighty palace was the House of Justice, one of several. A gate of figured bronze shone from the facade of the house. On the far side of the square, he could make out a loggia. It was dark in the loggia, and its darkness bristled.

He looked all about him and then moved with a wondering heart to the centre of the square. Turning round and round like a child, he gazed at the miraculous architecture with awestruck eyes. He breathed in the charmed open spaces. He drank in the blessed sky. He kept looking at everything, soaking in the strange enchantment of the air.

He felt as if he had stepped into the great old dreams he had heard tell about, where the dreamers find themselves in that place in all the universe where they feel most at home, and where their deepest nature can breathe and be free.

He felt he was in that place where he could step out of himself and into unbounded realms.

Sixteen

The truth was that he felt he had arrived at his life's true destination. He felt it as a mood of at-homeness. Then he felt that the longing for his true destination was itself the mood of the square.

Suddenly, he had an odd premonition. He sensed that his true destination was a place that he would eventually lose, would set out from, continuing his original search. Then, after finding what he wanted, and discovering that it wasn't what he really wanted, he would set out, on a sad quest, to the place he had lost, and would never find it again. He felt all this as in a dream.

At that moment, overcome with a dark happiness, he suddenly sensed that all the magic and the blessedness, the enchantment and the mystery, the wisdom of the civilisation and the majesty of the city, all were doomed. They were doomed the way beautiful things are doomed. But doomed in order to become higher, and last forever, in the places where things are most powerful and truly endure, in the living dreams of the universe.

Seventeen

He suspected, in a flash, how he too was doomed. But before he could reduce the intuition to a thought, he felt his guide leaving him. He felt his departing guide as a clear melody, a perfect enigma.

His mind became as anonymous as the night. Unfinished thoughts bristled in the dark loggias of his consciousness.

The guide, in his unique way, had passed on to him some things he needed to know. He had done this mysteriously, and in silence. The guide had made him hear them in the air, from the city stones, from the architecture, and from the streets. The guide had made the night speak to him.

The guide left without a farewell, and yet a sweetness lingered, as of sweet moments spent in the company of the serene and rich in spirit.

On that island, even the children were wise.

BOOK FOUR

One

He was standing there, alone, in the middle of the square, when he saw a mattress with white bedcovers brought to him in the dark. He didn't see the people who brought it, but they put the mattress on the stone floor of the square, dressed it neatly into a bed, and left. Soon afterwards unseen hands brought him a jug of water, a diamond glass for drinking, a rose, and a cluster of grapes. They set them down at the head of his bed. Then, not long afterwards, they brought him a lamp which glowed brightly, but whose glow created not illumination, but a deeper darkness. Then, finally, they brought him a mirror.

When they left, the square was silent again. Then the breeze blew through, stirring the memories of the stones, awakening the dreams of the open spaces, and reviving the darkened forms under the bristling loggias.

Two

The darkness was intense all around him because of the lamp's paradoxical glow, but farther away things were clearer. The square seemed bathed in a softly radiant moonlight.

He sat gently in the mystery of the square. He sat on his white bed, afloat in limpid moonlight. The palace loomed before him with its impenetrable walls and its massive gate. The great flag and its symbols fluttered in the gentle breeze, sending the hidden meaning of its sign and motto to all the regions of the mysterious land.

Three

He contemplated the overwhelming mystery of the square. He studied its bronze equestrian rider. He gazed upon its sea-god and horses emerging from a giant fountain of adamant. And he pondered its guardian figure of an ancient prophet-king who stood poised in dreaming marble before his own mystic annunciation of courage.

The equestrian rider was on a high diamond platform. With the hand bearing the shining sword of truth, he was pointing ever-forward to a great destiny and destination, never to be reached, because if reached the people and their journey would perish. He was pointing to an ever-moving destination, unspecified except in myth, the place of absolute self-realisation and contentment which must always be just beyond the reach of the brave land, but not so much beyond reach that the people would give up in perfection's despair, and set up tent somewhere between the sixth and final mountain.

The horse, with one mighty foot raised, was itself a sign and a dream. Its head was lofty and its eyes blazed with the will of the master.

The equestrian rider, massive, proud, and humble, was bathed in darkness, and partly hidden. It stood off the centre of the square. It was awkwardly placed, and yet remained the strange focus of all the geometric measurements and the astrological configurations. It always had to be rediscovered.

Four

The sea-god with his gleaming white steeds in the midst of the turbulent fountain was to the extreme left of the palace, and one of its guardians. He too was a dream and a sign. With his mighty beard and glistening trident, the sea-god seemed to be emerging from the depths of the ocean. The steeds, galloping on the churning waves, were resplendent. The sea-god, with trident held high, pointing to the immutable stars, was the ever-rising dream of the people's origins. He was the enactor of their resurrection from the terrors of the ocean bed. He seemed to bring with him a terrible light, from the unnameable source. The light he brings is absolute, difficult, and luminous.

Five

The figure of the prophet-king stands in the space between loggia and palace, and has stood there for centuries, old in time, young in myth, fresh in body. He stands at the inter-section between visibility and invisibility. He also stands at the moment before – the moment before he enters into legend.

Anxiety is etched on his brow. Supreme calm reigns over his face.

From the gleaming light of his body can be sensed the preparation in the fields, the solitude of the hills, the wrestling with demons, the music of the lyre, the eternal youth of the spirit, the happiness with nature, the angels visible in the mountains at night, and the voice of the unnameable in every rock and flower.

From the anxiety of his pose can be sensed kingship and weariness and old age of the spirit, fame and sad wars, temp-tations into which he will fall, and from which he will rise, life without the music of the lyre, without angels in the mountains, and without the whisperings of the unnameable in the trees and on the wind.

The prophet-king stands between loggia and palace, between visibility and invisibility, never crossing the line, caught in that moment, in beautiful marble, forever.

Six

And on a niche beside the palace gate, in purest stone, very small and humble, and yet encompassing the land with divinity, was the quiet figure of the great mother.

She was the lady of the mighty gate, protector of the land and its night.

Seven

He sat on his soft white bed, in the myth-soaked square, with its mood of ancient moonlight, and he was overcome with wonder. A strange yearning took hold of him. The sky opening above the square seemed a passage to the stars, to the dark universe. The brooding sky invited his soul to great adventures. He wanted to set sail again. He wanted to fly out into the mystery of that sky.

Then, while looking up, he noticed the most unusual thing. He noticed a sculpting which was itself invisible, and which became visible very briefly during certain moments of the day and night. The master sculptor of that land had long ago created a sculpting of the greatest Invisible of them all. It stood in midspace, just above the palace.

The levitating sculpture, finer than diamond, made of a material that seemed to be pure light, and yet as heavy as marble, rose higher into the air every year. It was a symbol and dream of the gentle master who had been visible to his followers for only three days before ascending into invisibility, and becoming one of the greatest forces for light in the spirit and imagination of the world.

He saw the sculpting high up in the air, unsupported. The light it gave off seemed to brighten the sky. He saw it briefly, and then it too was gone.

Eight

He was contemplating it all, very still, when he became aware of the bristling forms under the darkened loggia. When he looked harder, all he saw was the darkness stirring. But when he turned his head away he noticed for the first time that the statues of the loggia were beginning to move in the dark. He was so alarmed that he cried out in horror.

The night became still. Even the wind ceased.

The enchantment of the square suddenly changed for him, as if he had woken into a place whose horrors he hadn't previously noticed.

He stood up sharply, and listened.

Nine

At first, he heard nothing. Then, after a while, he heard a faint shuffling sound, and muffled cries of agony, as of a small animal dying.

He scanned the square, but saw nothing. The tiny shuffling noise continued moving towards him. He looked again, and saw nothing. The figures stirring in the loggia were still. The whole square was still, as if waiting. Then, just as he was about to sit down again, he saw it.

He saw it as a horrid worm, and as a monster – something evil that had crawled out from under the perfect stones. The world swam before his horrified gaze and a dryness filled his mouth. For a moment everything went dark about him and when he recovered himself, with his heart beating fast, he saw the creature crawling towards him in the dark. Somehow, it became perfectly visible, a mottled white against the patterned ochre of the stones. With faint cries of distress, it struggled on, crawling with great difficulty, pushing itself forward with its broken wings, and supporting itself on its one good foot. The other foot was bent and broken. It twitched in the soft moonlight.

For a long moment he watched the dove with a mixture of horror and fascination. For a long moment he didn't see it as a bird, but as a monster. The bird was crawling towards the

House of Justice, crawling there to die an honourable death.

But the moment he saw it as a bird struggling to get to the edge of the square, where there was a border of flowers, he also became aware of something else, something quite ominous.

Ten

He sensed that he was being watched. It seemed absurd to him, but it suddenly appeared that the square was crowded with people — people milling about, sitting at tables, under the moonlight, doing their normal everyday things, while being at the same time perfectly aware of him. He felt the square to be crowded, and yet he saw no one around. He also felt that he was being tested, and that whatever he did would determine his life on the new day.

He looked around again, and saw nothing, except the looming palace, the silent square, and the empty ancient spaces.

The bird had crawled past him, uttering its low pathetic noises, pushing on with its broken wings. He felt great pity for the bird and wondered why no one helped it, or cared for it, or took it home to heal, even when he knew perfectly well that there was no one around except him.

He felt great pity for the bird, but for a while he didn't move. He didn't do anything. Moments passed. Suddenly, he couldn't bear it any longer, and went towards the dove.

Just as he was about to crouch and investigate the nature of its wound, he became aware of someone standing beside him. Standing silently, not breathing.

Eleven

He let out a gasp of shock, and jumped backwards, the world reeling in his eyes. When he recovered from his shock he saw the dark form of a tall lean youth standing there. The lean youth was also regarding the white dove.

'His companions did this to him,' said the lean figure, in a dry sepulchral voice.

'What companions?'

'His companions. They did this. They fell on him and broke his wings. They tried to kill him. They knew he couldn't make the journey.'

There was silence. After a while, during which the breeze stirred in the square, ruffling the mane of the great rider's horse, the lean figure said:

'Can you hear what the dove is crying?'

'No.'

'Can't you hear what he is crying?'

'No.'

'Can't you hear at all?'

'No.'

'You can't hear anything?'

'Yes, of course. I can hear its noise of distress.'

'You mean pain?'

'Yes, pain.'

'And you can't hear what the pain is saying?'

'No, of course not. Any why are you asking me all these questions anyway? Why don't you do something about the poor bird, instead of just standing there and talking?'

The figure, drily, replied:

'Well, I was about to. But you seemed concerned as well. What were you going to do?'

'I don't know.'

There was another silence. Then, leaning forward ever so slightly, the figure said:

'This is what the pain is saying: Either give me life, or kill me.'

'I don't understand.'

'The bird is saying: Either heal me, or kill me.'

'Well, I can't kill it.'

'Then you must give it life.'

'I don't know how to give it life.'

'You don't?'

'No.'

'Then what are you doing here?'

'Where?'

'Here. On this island, in this square, at this moment.'

'I don't know.'

'You don't know?'

'No.'

'How odd.'

'There's nothing odd about it. I am here. There's a reason why, but I don't know the reason.'

'So you can't give life?'

'No. And what about you? What were you going to do? You clearly feel pity for the bird.'

The figure looked at him with an intense sort of vacancy. At that moment he became aware that there was another figure behind the tall lean youth. It was a female form. She stepped from behind the first figure, silently. He couldn't make out her face. They both seemed to have been made out of the same dark and obscure material. The first figure leant over, picked up the bird, and was about to break its neck, but stopped suddenly.

'I am going to kill it,' the figure said, without any emotion. 'It will die anyway. It won't last the night. There is no point in prolonging its agony. And it is cruel to leave it out in the square, shivering and suffering a long, slow, and lingering death. Meanwhile, you would be comfortably asleep in your bed. I am going to kill it.'

'Don't.'

'Why not?'

'Would you like that done to you?'

The figure paused and seemed to think about it. After a long moment, he turned to the other form, his female companion, and they talked in low voices. When they had finished, he turned back and said:

'Just one twist of the neck, that's all. And it will all be over.'

'Don't.'

'Can you give it life?'

'I don't know how to give life.'

'All these years of being alive and you haven't learned?'

'No.'

'If you can't give it life, then you must kill it.'

'I can't kill it.'

'Then I will kill it.'

'You mustn't.'

'There is nothing for me to do. I can't heal it. I can't give it life. That is my profound and regrettable failure. But I can give it death. I can end its misery. There is compassion in that too. A lesser compassion, I concede, but better than leaving it to die in the open air, alone. There's nothing for me to do. You won't let me kill it, so I now hand it over to you. I have done my best. It's now up to you. But you must give it life, or kill it. There is no middle way. You can't be neutral on this. The responsibility is yours. Goodnight.'

Whereupon the tall lean figure put the dove back on the stone floor and, linking hands with the female form, disappeared into the night.

The bird went on crawling, flailing, uttering its plaintive cry.

He stood there, watching it helplessly. And then, without thinking, he went over and picked up the dying bird. He was slightly frightened by its fragile bones and its twitching wings. He took it back with him to the bed.

He placed the dove beside his pillow, and lay down, and caressed it, saying:

'How is it that I have never learned how to give new life?'

Twelve

The thought made him very unhappy; for now he had a terrible choice to make. He had no ability to kill. He had never killed a thing in his life. He had never watched a living thing die. He had never healed anything either.

Now, he had to heal or kill.

And the bird was past normal healing. It would require a miracle. The concept of a miracle was strange to him, strange and wonderful and oddly terrifying.

He cuddled the bird closer to him, and soon fell asleep.

Thirteen

When he woke up, the bird was gone. The night was somehow darker, and the square brooded in deeper mystery. He looked around for the dying bird, and was distressed at not being able to find it. The thought that while he slept the bird had somehow got past his protective arm and crawled to some corner and was dying there filled him with a vague sense of guilt.

He had failed to make a decision and, deciding now, he got up from the bed and went searching the corners of the square, searching in the direction of the House of Justice, where the bird had originally been heading. He searched the herbaceous borders, and couldn't find it. He looked amongst the flowers, but it wasn't there. He had no idea how long he had been sleeping. The bird might have died by now.

He was searching somewhat frantically for the dove when he saw someone coming down from the platform of the darkened loggia. It was a thin, tiny figure, with a large head. One moment the figure was at the loggia; and the next moment, somewhat transformed in stature, the figure stood near the flowers, watching him silently.

'Who are you? Where did you come from?'

'Me?' the figure said. 'My name is unimportant, like all names. And I dwell in the loggia. Why do you ask?'

'Well, I was surprised to see you.'

'I've been watching you all night.'

'Why?'

'You were there to watch.'

He went on looking for the dove.

'Whatever it is you are looking for can't be found,' the dwarf-like figure said.

'Why not?'

'In this place if you look for something you won't find it.'

'Why is that?'

'You have to find things first before you look for them.'

'You're talking nonsense.'

'It's true. The laws of this place are strange.'

'Explain yourself.'

'Well, it's like this. If you are looking for something, that means you have lost it. And if you have lost it, you can't find it. Quite simple.'

The breeze stirred again, darkening the large-headed figure, who remained dwarf-like and still and massive.

'I don't think that's simple at all. In fact, it's quite complicated.'

'Well, look at it this way. You shouldn't have lost it in the first place.'

'You mean if you lose something you can't find it?'

'Yes.'

'But what if for once I do?'

'You wouldn't have found the same thing.'

'You're being perverse.'

'Not at all. You only have one chance here. If you have something, keep it, be aware of it, treasure it, enrich it. Because, here, if you lose it then you didn't have it in the first place. You weren't aware of it. You didn't guard it. You didn't give it life. And so it wasn't real for you. In this place things lose their reality if you are not aware of them.'

The breeze was silent now. The square seemed to have changed a little, as if it were fading, or receding, or disappearing into the silence.

The dwarf-like figure continued.

'Take me, for example. I kept looking for the answer to things. I kept looking, and I never saw, and I became lost. I lost myself, lost my own reality. So I should know.'

'But how can I find without looking?'

'You will never find by looking. You have to find first. Take me, for example. Too late I discovered that the answers were always there. Always.'

'And you never found them?'

'No.'

'Why not?'

'Because I was looking for them. How can you look for something that is there?'

'I suppose you can't.'

'Of course you can't. Things only disappear, only become lost, because you've stopped thinking about them, stopped living with them in some vital way. Things and people have to be planted in you, have to grow in you, and you have to keep them alive. If you forget to keep them alive, you lose them. Many people have walked out of life because they stopped seeing it. Many have fallen into the abyss because they were looking for solid ground, for certainties. Happy are those who are still, and to whom things come. Answers are like that. They go to those who expect them. So, if you want to find something find it first.'

'How?'

'Find it in yourself, I suppose.'

'You talk in riddles.'

'The simplest things are riddles and paradoxes. Have you heard about people looking for love?'

'Yes.'

'They never find love, do they?'

'I don't know.'

'They never find the love they are looking for.'

'I'm not so sure.'

'Those who find love find it in themselves.'

'I suppose so.'

'It is so. I should know.'

'Why?'

'Because I looked for and never found love. I found something else.'

'What?'

'Something that looked like love, but wasn't. Others I know never looked and they found. They found it in abundance. For them it was always there. Love was always alive in them. It was always there.'

'Where?'

'Everywhere. They merely invited it, and it came. They merely were, and it was attracted. Love goes to where love is. And where love is, love is never lost. Lucky are those who know how to find, for they will never lose things.'

Fourteen

There was a short pause during which he studied the dwarf-like figure, trying to clarify its strangely shifting form. The figure, short and enigmatic and still, began to move away.

'Don't go,' he said.

'I have to,' the figure replied.

'I am alone here. I don't understand anything. This place is new to me, its ways are odd, and I have no one to talk to. My bed is over there. I have some water, some grapes, and would gladly share them with you.'

'I have no need of water or grapes,' said the figure, 'but I'll keep you company for a while. I must be back at the loggia at an appointed time.'

They went towards the bed. The dwarf-like figure brought its darkness with it, and even under the moonlight remained obscure. The figure had a heavy tread, as if it were made not of flesh but of adamant, or ancient marble.

He sat on the bed, poured himself some water, and drank from the diamond glass. The large-headed figure remained standing. It stood in its own darkness. After a while, the figure spoke.

'Why are you here?'

'I left my home seeking to be visible.'

'You came to the wrong place. Here things are invisible. The real things can't be seen.'

'But I feel at peace here.'

'You won't for long.'

'Why not?'

'Because what you are seeking isn't here. There are many lands beyond, where people know true peace. They know contentment. They never seek, never search. They have all that they want. They are visible, and their lands ring with happiness. That's what you want.'

'That sounds like here.'

'Not here. You should follow your seeking to the end.'

'But you said if I look I'll never find.'

'That's true of everything except what I just told you.'

'You contradict yourself.'

'No I don't. You seek visibility. Here, things are invisible. You are therefore in the wrong place. Quite simple.'

'I feel in the right place though.'

'Then you are not seeking to be visible, you are not seeking visibility.'

'I was.'

'You still are. Your trouble is that you don't know this place. This is a rigorous land. Everyone lives without illusions. It is exhausting. One can't live in perfection the whole time. Purity, after a while, is boring. Too much invisibility can mean you stop existing. Even the wind wants to be visible. To be invisible is like living with your own death all the time. Who wants to be always dead. To be visible is to live with your life, your mortality. It is to be alive, to see and be seen. You're in the wrong place. It won't be long before you go completely mad.'

'Mad?'

'Yes. You'd go mad. You'd start seeing things. Invisible things. You'd see them in mirrors. You'd see them in the air. A cart would rush past with no one pushing it. Horses would disappear. The wind would become a woman. You'd start to talk to people who aren't there. You'd start to hear voices. Mad, yes, quite mad. Then, worst of all, you'd start looking for things and end up looking for yourself. In the end you'd scream for visibility and you'd flee this island, crying out for places where people have names and where you can participate in some useful struggle and where there are a thousand useful and beautiful illusions.'

'So what should I do?'

'Quite simple, really. Leave now. Don't delay. The longer you remain, the more invisible you will become. Leave. Depart. Go to better places, where visibility is bliss.'

'What do I do?'

'Easy. Simple. All you have to do is go now and knock on the palace door. Knock, it will be opened. Then tell them you want to leave. Or you can merely start to scream your desire to be visible now. Then they will come and take you away. Very simple.'

'But what if I like it here?'

'Believe me, you wouldn't like it here for long. Soon the excessive beauty would make you miserable. It would become like hell, an inferno of perfections. Imagine it: a hell made out of beauty. Can you think of anything more stultifying, more suffocating, than a nightmare composed entirely of beautiful things, of flowers, and pure lights, and mirrors? And the worst would be that you would become trapped here, like me, forever.'

'You make it sound chilling.'

'It is chilling. It is more chilling than I can make it sound. Leave now while you can. Be free of this impossible place, this rigorous land, where everything is guided by the wisdom of suffering, and where the journey towards perfection is continued without any hope of ever arriving. Find joy! Live your life! Make your mistakes! Enjoy life's illusions! Don't become invisible, don't turn to stone. Don't seek impossible loves, find possible ones! Leave now, knock on that palace door, and soon you will find yourself where you belong. Soon you will arrive at the destination you've been seeking since you left your home.'

Fifteen

He thought about what the figure had been saying. For a moment he was convinced. The square was all mist now, receding into the wind. All he could see was the palace door and the dazzling sword of the equestrian rider, pointing towards an eternal destination.

The darkness around the dwarf-like figure had grown massive. The darkness grew as his doubts waned. Then, all of a sudden, the figure moved. Without knowing why, he thought of his first guide. He looked about him. The square became clearer, with the sea-god emerging from the billowing marble waves.

He said:

'This place has not been unkind to me. I saw my first unicorn today. I even saw an angel. I think I'll have some more water and some grapes. You have been a most interesting companion.'

There was a long silence. The figure, eventually, said:

'The door is always there.'

'I won't lose it.'

'So you prefer to stay?'

'The grapes will last me all night. The square is peaceful. And I haven't yet enjoyed this bed.'

'You prefer to betray the deep thing that made you leave your home?'

'I don't know what I have found.'

'Then you can't be saved.'

'Perhaps not. I am touched that you think I am worthy of being saved. Thank you for trying.'

The massive figure watched him silently. Everything was still.

He bent over, and helped himself to some grapes. And when he looked up, the figure was gone.

There was stillness in the darkness of the loggia.

The wind was fragrant.

The square had survived the eclipsing mist. And moonlight made everything shimmer.

'That's two things I have to learn,' he said to himself. 'I have to learn how to give life, and I have to learn how to find.'

Sixteen

He was eating of the grapes, breathing deeply of the rose-flavoured wind, when a woman came to him out of the moon-light. He couldn't see her face clearly, but he felt her to be of extreme beauty, full in body, rich in sensuality, but obscure. He didn't know what was obscure about her.

She sat beside him on the bed and her presence affected him deeply. Her body breathed out an unbearable lustful air. So strong was her lust that he began to quiver. Baring her thighs to him casually, she said:

'I have hungered for a man such as you for many long years. Do you know what it is like when your body and soul crave a particular person whom you have not met, but whom you sense exists, and for whom you have been waiting for hundreds of years? Sensitive lovers know this feeling. We call it: "Sickness for your Orpheus". That's what I've had. You are my Orpheus. In my dreams I have loved you and wanted you. There has been no other, and there never will be. You are my missing soul. To be in your presence alone is like having entered a fairy-tale. I am a princess again, and you are my missing prince. Under these skies, in this square that has suffered more history than it has known love, and with the wind fragrant with a moment that will never be repeated, I have found you just as I thought I would – on a white bed, in the marble square, with a jug of water, and eating the grapes of the king.'

Seventeen

She moved closer to him as his eyes shut gently under the spell of her words. But more powerful than her words was her desire. It overwhelmed him. It made the blood sing in his ears. Her lust filled the spaces about him and changed the night into something infinitely sensual. He found himself unable to breathe. Her lust had somehow infected him.

Looking at her out of eyes changed by transferred desire, he noticed that she was attired in a soft golden shift. Her legs were graceful and sensuous. Her rich breasts lightly heaved. Her lips were ripe and full, like summer grapes. She was a paradoxical beauty, full-bodied and classical, chaste and wild. The combination was irresistible.

She had moved so close to him that he no longer breathed air. He breathed in her lust, her charged fragrance, and her fiery sensuality. The mystery of her in that square made him think of frenzied journeys driven by the face of a woman who was somehow the meaning of his life. He saw in her that woman. He stayed silent. She began again to speak.

'Do you not recognise me?'

'I think I do,' he replied, 'but it would be strange if I said so.'

'Fate is strange,' she mused. 'We plan our lives according to a dream that came to us in our childhood, and we find that life alters our plans. And yet, at the end, from a rare height, we also see that our dream was our fate. It's just that providence had other ideas as to how we would get there. Destiny plans a different route, or turns the dream around, as if it were a riddle, and fulfills the dream in ways we couldn't have expected. How far back is our childhood? Twenty years? Thirty? Fifty? Or ten? I think our childhood goes back thousands of years, farther back than the memory of any race. When we yearn, our yearning comes through from deep below. It comes from a deep remembering, from the forgotten dreams of our mingled ancestry. You are my yearning. And this is the night, long ago, when our stars first met. They are together now, in the heavens, shedding a beautiful radiance on this night. They are weaving enchantments for us so that we may step through the invisible mirror in the air and enter the fairy-tale we are meant to live, but which we forgot.'

Eighteen

The extraordinary lady paused, then continued:

'Are you comfortable? Are you all right? Is the wind too cold for you? Should I go and fetch you some more fruits? I love your silence. It is so wise. It listens. It invites warmth. I love your loneliness. It is brave. It makes the universe want to protect you. You have the loneliness that all true heroes have, a loneliness that is a deep sea, within which the fishes of mystery dwell. I love your quest. It is noble. It has greatness in it. Only one who is born under a blessed star would set sail across the billowing waves and the wild squalls, because of a dream. I love your dream. It is magical. Only those who truly love and who are truly strong can sustain their lives as a dream. You dwell in your own enchantment. Life throws stones at you, but your love and your dream change those stones into the flowers of discovery. Even if you lose, or are defeated by things, your triumph will always be exemplary. And if no one knows it, then there are places that do. People like you enrich the dreams of the world, and it is dreams that create history. People like you are unknowing transformers of things, protected by your own fairy-tale, by love. If it weren't for this overpowering love of mine, I would praise you better.'

Nineteen

Suddenly, she began weeping. She wept in silence, without moving. He watched her with the moon in his heart.

When she stopped, he started to speak, but she signalled him to be silent.

'My love for you makes me so unhappy,' she said, gently. 'All these years of yearning have filled me with an unhappy wisdom. May I lie down beside you?'

'Yes,' he replied, without knowing why.

She lay down beside him and her lust spread a curious darkness over the bed. He seemed to be afloat in her desire. He seemed to levitate in her passion. He surrendered his senses to her power. Gently, she made him lie down. Then she whispered these words into his ear:

'I am the mystery that will unlock your life.'

Twenty

Her words made him drowsy. He shut his eyes. When he opened them again he found her naked beside him.

Drawn by the irresistible charm of her flesh, he was moving his hand towards her rich breasts, when the breeze stirred again, gently obliterating the square.

For a moment a yellow mist filled the open spaces. The equestrian rider seemed to be lost in an appalling fog. Not even his pointed sword was visible. The sea-god was entirely swallowed by the mist. And his steeds, struggling vainly, could not emerge from the yellow pall.

The palace itself was now a thing discernible only by its dim battlements and its flag, barely fluttering in the breeze, sending its sign all around the city. The mist had climbed the high walls and softened the face of its stone. The palace seemed to be dissolving under the passion of the yellow fog.

Only the head of the prophet-king was visible, and his anxiety seemed more pronounced.

Again she whispered into his ears.

'I will give you all the secrets of life on this special night. Everything you need to know is within me. Are you comfortable? Do you see how everything is succumbing to our dream? Will you make love to me? I desire you to do so. I desire that we share one another's mystery.'

Without saying another word she entangled him with her hot legs, entangled him with her beautiful lust. Her loins were warm, and her breasts trembled. He caressed her soft and voluptuous body. She drew him closer and pressed him into the wild warmth of her breasts.

But just as their lips were going to meet and merge, he noticed that the square was now totally obscure. The marble floor, the palace gate, the distant spires, the head of the prophet-king, were all now in yellow darkness. Only the loggia seemed the same.

Twenty-One

Without knowing why, touched by a breeze which brought unspoken words from the abyss beneath the invisible bridge, he pulled back from the passion of the mysterious woman. He sat up straight, shook his head vigorously, and said:

'Please accept this rose from me as a token of profound gratitude. Your words have moved me more than I can say. And your love – your love is wonderful.'

He picked up the rose from where it lay, next to the diamond glass. He offered it to her with a smile. She accepted it silently.

In a different voice, full of sadness and compassion, and yet quite firm, he said:

'The night was enchanted, but now it is filled with mist. It was a fairy-tale, but now it is tender and yellow. I don't understand. But this much I do know. I think I am lucky. Today, I managed to cross an abyss without a bridge. And today I met you. And you are unique. You are incomparable. You are a poet and a princess. You have been very kind to me and have said such sweet words as would make a statue of marble writhe with passion. Your longing is too great for me. Your beauty is terrifying. It already says goodbye. It sets the night on fire, and I am merely someone in a square, on a bed, with water and grapes, waiting for dawn. I don't want the secret of things from you. It is a generous offer. But I have the secret of things already, somewhere. Besides, someone told me on this same night that I must learn to find. Thank you for your company, for your warmth, for the gift of your words. But, if you don't mind, I must resume waiting for dawn, alone.'

Twenty-Two

The woman stared at him for a long time. The wind had changed. Slowly, the square re-emerged from the yellow mist, the equestrian rider resumed his motionless journey, and the prophet-king re-entered the moment between anxiety and legend.

After a long silence, the mysterious woman got out of the bed. She came up close to him. Her face was still obscure. She said:

'Because you rejected my love, this is my curse on you. Refusing to love an illusion, you will have to love without illusion. I cannot think of anything more cheerless. You will live to regret the night you rejected the advances of a famous princess like me.'

After she had spoken, she strode away with a proud and splendid sensuality. She strode out into the moonlight, taking her obscurities and yellow darkness with her.

Twenty-Three

When she had gone, he spread himself out on the bed. He drank some more water from the diamond glass, and ate some more grapes. The world was now restored. Everything fairly glowed. There was a faint radiance in the air. The marble floor shimmered. The wind murmured. A gentle melody rose from beneath all things. The palace was bathed in a new light, a clear new light that sharpened its edges. It appeared now in an eternal freshness, remade in its own lucid dream. The sky was youthful and clear, as on the first day of its creation. And from its far corner, dawn was gently reclaiming the long mystery of that night.

Thinking about the strange woman, he reached for some more grapes, and noticed something peculiar about the mirror. Before he tucked himself into bed, he picked up the mirror and looked into it. He was surprised to find his features fading, disappearing. At first it occurred to him that he was exhausted, and that his eyes were tired. But, overcome with an oddly repellent notion, he put the mirror down hurriedly.

He thought about many things. He was mildly disturbed. He thought about the woman again.

'That's something else I will have to learn,' he said to himself. 'I will have to learn to love without illusion.'

Then he turned over and fell soundly asleep.

BOOK FIVE

BOOK FIVE

One

Early in the morning he was awoken by the voice of another woman. He couldn't see her. She was his new guide. She was very gentle. Her voice was warm with compassion and light. He could have sworn that the sound of her voice, mysterious in the empty space from which it emanated, conjured up her physical presence. He knew that she was astonishing, and that her beauty faced inwards. He submitted himself to her tender guidance.

Taking him by the hand, so that he nearly jumped out of himself for the thrill of her lovely touch, she led him to the room of purification. He was made to bathe. Fresh clothes of rich brocade and satin and gold-tricked silk appeared to him in the air. He wore them, and waited.

Then he was led to another room. There he sat silently at the emerald shrine. The golden image of the sun, with its omnipresent and compassionate eye, looked kindly upon him.

He sat in silence, patiently, till his guide came and led him across the square. She led him past the loggia. Amongst the many statues he noticed those of a broad-shouldered dwarf, a famous loving couple, and a celebrated princess of antiquity. When they got to the palace gate, his guide departed with a sigh.

The gate was shut. He didn't know what to do. Turning

around he saw, not far from him, the figure of the prophet-king on his marble pedestal. Looking up at the face of the prophet-king, he was struck by how serene he was. His anxiety concealed his serenity. And his serenity gave him an eternal beauty, as if his essential spirit was forever at ease with Time and the universe. When he looked more carefully, he also noticed that at the heart of that serenity was a smile. The smile was the secret of the prophet-king's legend.

He was still thinking about that concealed smile, which seemed to come from a deep place and which barely made itself visible on his face, when the great door of the palace opened ceremoniously before him.

Sweet pipe music, the whisperings of a happy flute, and the stirring call of harmonious trumpets sounded gently from within. Then a melodious voice said:

'Come in you who would enter the palace. Step over the silver line of the humble gate.'

He went in, and the door shut behind him.

Two

He found himself in complete darkness. There was the aroma of frankincense in the air. He stood in the darkness for a long time. Slowly, be became aware that he could no longer see himself. His physical presence had succumbed to the darkness. He had disappeared. For a moment he too was invisible to himself. He nearly screamed.

The darkness dissolved his existence. After a while he was no longer sure if he was there or not. He wasn't even sure if he was standing on solid ground or floating above an abyss. He felt himself floating. He felt parts of himself being obliterated by the darkness. His mind became empty. It too was invaded by the complete blackness.

Then he became conscious of the silence. The silence and the blackness cancelled him out completely.

Soon he was adrift in an empty universe, without light, and without sound.

He might as well have died.

Three

He tried to move, but couldn't. He tried to think, but couldn't either. Invisibility had conquered his mind. He was overcome with a sort of sublime horror.

Then, suddenly, a colossal voice, thundering all over the palace, as if a god were speaking, said:

'WHAT IS THE MYSTERY OF THE BRIDGE?'

The voice could have destroyed him. It certainly made him jump deeper into the dark places, utterly fragmenting his being.

His heart stopped beating.

A long moment passed in this terror.

'WHAT IS THE MYSTERY OF THE BRIDGE?' the voice thundered again, quaking the palace and its deep foundations, and rocking him into the most terrifying silences of the universe.

Another long moment passed in this stillness.

He was now so tiny in that dark space that to himself he ceased to exist.

The question was asked a third time. And the voice, booming from the sky, made the whole city shake.

Then he was overwhelmed by blinding lights of ultramarine and topaz, of gold and polished bronze. The streaming radiance of stained-glass windows and the dancing beams of sunlit diamonds opened on him suddenly, enveloping him as if he had emerged upon the open fields of heaven and been embraced by a luminous host of angels.

The beauty of the lights was so awesome that he collapsed at the threshold of the palace.

Four

Everywhere he looked he saw images of perfection. Angels were flying through the air and the most beautiful women in all creation were emerging from the waves of the purest seas. Glorious colours were all around. He found himself in the early days, among the earliest heroes of the Invisibles, at the first foundation of the golden age. He found himself with them, rising from the sea-bed, embarking on the building of their universal civilisation.

He was with the splendid array of men and women in their early battles with the darkness and monsters of the island. He was among them, building their bridges of light, their mighty cathedrals, their emerald towers, their architecturally perfect abodes, their marble roads. He was among them, conquering the marshes, constructing their houses of justice, their market-places and loggias, shaping their streets, designing the spirit-ual symmetry of their cities and towns, creating their holy places, filling their mountains with shrines, carving beautiful statues all over their hill tops, building canals, developing the sciences, planting flowers in their magical gardens, and inventing labyrinths which at regular seasons formed their arcane symbol of eternity.

There was harmony and spring everywhere. There was a difficult joy and a difficult light in the early heroic days. There were no hierarchies. Each person was an equal participant and creator. All worked to the rhythm of the most haunting music, a music full of sorrow and rich with hope. Together they built their towns and hamlets, their palaces and villas, their avenues of angels, their infinite libraries, their exemplary universities. There were no distinctions between people, none high, none low, and men fed children while women constructed temples. There was suffering and a profound vision on all their faces.

He was among them when they discovered the unnameable in the mountains, when the angels pointed the way to their destiny, when the sages and prophets were inspired by the laws of life which the seraphs brought on emerald tablets, and when the dreams of their distant future were revealed to them. His heart too was glorious with amazement and humility.

He was there when miraculous fountains spouted from the rocks and when signs were given from heaven about how they could transform their terror and their great suffering into beauty.

He was also there on the great day when all the people, freshly risen from the ocean bed, gathered on the occasion of the great covenant, the momentous event of the consecration of their master dream. It was a day of the most beautiful rituals. It was the day when the people promised to the heavens that out of their agony they would make a wonderful destiny. With the sweetest and most solemn vows, they pledged to create a civilisation of light and justice. They pledged to initiate on earth the first universal civilisation where love and wisdom would be as food and air.

On that great day a marvellous sign came upon the people. As the rituals were coming to an end, there was an extra-ordinary flash of light in the sky. Then the heavens, as if in a mysterious annunciation, revealed their splendours and their luminous glories. And when the people freshly arisen from the ocean bed looked upwards, they saw a fabulous sight. They saw themselves mirrored in heaven. They saw the shining doubles of themselves, clothed in the miraculous light of perfection.

To realise a little of heaven on earth, that was the glory of their promise.

The beauty of that moment was overwhelming. Suddenly, looking about him, he saw poets dancing with angels, musicians levitating over happy pastoral scenes, scientists discovering unknown sacred places.

He saw them all. He was with them all in the world of moving frescoes that quivered in that august hall.

BOOK SIX

One

It took some time before he discovered that he was in an august hall, dazzled by the miraculous lights of an ancient dawn.

While he slowly came back to himself from the masterful images arrayed on the walls, his guide touched his hand and said:

'You'd better go to your seat. All the illustrious ones are present. And all are waiting for you to find your place before the ceremony can begin.'

That was when he first became aware that the vast hall was crowded. It was crowded with invisible presences. They were there, sitting in chairs, in neat rows, all the way from the great door to the marble podium. Their collective presence electrified the hall. They shimmered in their empty spaces like the air after lightning.

On the podium there was a long silver table. Behind the table, buntings and banners, held aloft by the invisible city guild, hung proudly, displaying the mystic signs of the city's motto and heraldic emblem.

He gazed in astonishment at the shining spaces. He was overwhelmed by the heightened mood in the august hall, by the radiant presences, the serene air, the deep-sea calm, the mountain solidity, and the blue wisdom that surrounded him in the ritual moment. He realised suddenly how all the lights in the spaces filled the hall with an intangible mood of divinity.

'You are in the presence of the illuminators. These are the guardians of the spiritual realms, protectors of the secret of secrets.'

So saying, his guide led him gently but firmly down the aisle, past the empty chairs occupied by noble and enlightened beings, and all the way to the front row. Hurriedly, as the drums and trumpets began to sound by themselves, played by invisible masters, she made him sit down.

When he sat, he felt the masters all about him. He heard their murmurs and their muted conversations. If he hadn't looked back he would have felt them as a hall crowded with beings. But when he did look back, he heard the voices but saw nothing. The eerie sensation of being in a great hall full of people he couldn't see filled him with an enchanted unease. It was as if they were in a separate realm, a hidden dimension. In order to make sense of the uneasy sensation he had to imagine himself blind. With his eyes shut, he made an astonishing discovery. They became real. They acquired individuality. And when they spoke, invisible though they were, their voices conjured to him aspects of their personalities.

And so, blind among the empty chairs, he suddenly could see. That was when he first became aware of the splendid and miraculous lives of the Invisibles.

Two

He listened to the resonant speeches from the platform and realised that he couldn't understand what was being said. He noticed however that the uttered words transformed the air.

The first master of the long table spoke slowly, and his words induced a great calm over the hall. A wind of peace blew over from the words, spreading warmth and extending the spaces. Soon the hall seemed very vast. The words began to resonate from the magical frescoes.

The first master created a landscape filled with peaceful spirits, with a faun playing a pan-pipe, and a white horse galloping up the first mountain, and the leaves of the trees glistening under a heavenly light.

The words began to alter the hall, began to so expand the spaces that, sitting in the front row, he suddenly felt himself surrounded by benign presences in an expanse of light. He seemed utterly alone in the blue dazzling lights of the vast hall.

And then, out of the words, music began playing. He listened to the ritual music, to its bells and flutes and pan-pipes and violins, its tinkling harmonies, its soaring pastoral mood.

And he became aware, as he listened, that he was now in a different place. He dwelled there for a long time, not knowing where it was, but sensing that he was being raised up, being changed, as he lingered.

When he came to himself there was a new silence all about and he realised that the first master had finished and that he hadn't understood. He was about to turn his head towards the seat next to him, where his female guide was supposed to be, when the hall erupted in applause and joyful acclamation.

Three

After a long pause, the second master began speaking. Still he couldn't understand. Then as he listened he noticed again how the words were altering the hall.

Diamond lights shimmered from the words and spangles of emerald sunlight danced about the place, dwelling briefly and intensely on every person in the hall. And when the sunlight dwelled on him he shouted and nearly burst out of his body for the sheer beatification of his being.

Then a tender aroma of honeysuckle wafted out of the words, charming the air. Then a gentle incense wove its way round the invisible personages. And then an odour of boundless seas, of those spaces between water and sky where all is perpetually purified by the winds of heaven, blew in rhythmic waves through the hall.

And then he realised that he was somewhere else, in an eternal room of meditation, amongst the most magical thoughts and enchanted silences in the world.

The thoughts converged there from all realms. And each thought had infinite possibilities. He could have dwelled in any single one of those magical thoughts for a lifetime and not realised its full potential. Each of the thoughts, simple and clear like a drop of pure water, or a moment in a dream, revolved silently, and filled the room, and co-existed with all the others. The thoughts came from stones and seraphs, from trees and birds, from beings who dwelled in the air and beings who dwelled beyond the air, from human beings all over the world and beings in all the other spheres, from the dreams of the living and the continued meditations of the dead, from sea and cloud, from spirit and star, the thoughts came, and they went through him and left no imprints, and he noticed how small the room was for such crowded infinities.

And the enchanted silences converged there too from all realms. And each of the silences also had infinite possibilities and magnification without end. He could have lived in any of the silences for a millennium and not exhausted its mystery. Each of the silences, vast and serene, like a moment on the highest mountain, or a gentle breeze within a mirror, permeated the room, and dwelled at ease with all the others. The silences came from mountaintops covered with snow and the depths of unfathomed oceans, from the face of the moon and the forests at night, from the stalagmites of green caves and the axis of constellations, from human beings in their lonely places and beings in their higher spaces, from the dreams of a newborn babe and the first moments of emerging flowers, from angels and diamonds, from the heart of Time and the languid countrysides, from the hidden dimensions and the hidden heaven, from all the dead and all whose hearts quicken to the highest love, the silences came, and they passed through him, and they altered no spaces, and he noticed how real the room of meditations was for such dancing eternities.

Then, as he was about to stand up and begin dancing himself in nameless joy, he was stunned by another eruption of applause and exultation. He found himself back in the august hall again. The hall quaked under the rousing reception all the Invisibles were giving the second master. He still hadn't understood what was said.

Bewildered now, and puzzled by the way in which the words were altering the universe about him, he turned to the empty space where his female guide was, and said:

'Maybe you can explain.'

But all he got by way of an explanation was a touch of such tenderness that he was amazed by the momentary simplicity of everything.

He didn't have long to dwell in that moment's understanding when the third master of the silver table began to speak.

Four

The words of the third master were melodious and they filled the hall with music.

Out of the words flowed notes of perfect resolution, sonatas of joy, limpid moments between delightful chords, the laughter of a happy child, the serenity of light rain at midnight, a city at peace with its greatness, unheard notes on the musical scale, bird-calls at dawn, glittering ideas in sound, the vision of beautiful things flowering from great suffering, the hint of a grand and majestic aria flowing across the faces of the mountaintops and at rest on the gentle bed of the oceans, a song spiralling towards an unseen silver sphere, a praise of invisible things that are irresistible and supreme for being invisible, the blissful realm of the purest dreams, a tower of light, a river of sweet melodies, a calling forth of hidden things, the tranquillity that has gone beyond life and death, a white stairway climbing into the heavens, and the humour of those who are at home with their destiny.

All of this, and more, flowed out of the hidden music of the third master's words and out of the melody of his voice. And, as the third master spoke on, the hall was suddenly abolished, its walls rendered invisible, and the new space was radiant with the appearance of a summoned being, the tender presence of the great mother, protectress of the island and its secret ways.

The swirling energies of this being were everywhere, making the spaces alive with something akin to the electrification of the spirit, and a mighty collective hum of praise burst forth from the congregation of the illuminators. The hall now seemed to have lifted off into the air, and the city seemed in flight. Such a splendid weightlessness pervaded everything, and all those in the great hall seemed to be afloat on a silver cloud, spiralling into the soaring sublimity of the great mother.

It wasn't long before he felt that something about him had changed forever in that celestial mood. He felt that he had become smaller and therefore greater, that he had become hidden and therefore could learn to see, that he had become a secret and therefore open to all truths, that he had become his own mystery and therefore could begin to understand, and that he had been touched by the creative spirit of finding and therefore could begin his true quest.

And while still afloat in that heavenly mood, he became aware that something had changed around him too. He noticed the deep blue silence and realised that the third master had finished.

The silence was the applause, the highest applause, that the congregation of the Invisibles could have given to one of their most venerable illuminators.

BOOK SEVEN

One

The silence after the third master's speech went on for a long time. Everything seemed to dissolve in that long silence. It was so profound that, for a moment, he was no longer sure if anyone was actually around. He felt that he was alone and insane in a vast empty hall.

And then the silence changed. It became the silence of all the Invisibles in contemplation of their great dream and destiny. This was one of their favoured forms of making visions real.

The silence went on so long that he became frightened. He felt himself disintegrating. Then, as he began to panic at the duration of the stillness, he became aware that the silence was speaking to him. The silence said many things beyond his comprehension, and what he heard were the lesser things. And the silence spoke to him, saying:

'Time is different here. We measure time differently, not by the passing of moments or hours, but by lovely deeds, creative accomplishments, beautiful transformations, by little and great perfections.

'Size is also measured differently here. For us something is great if it is beautiful, if it is true, and if it has life. Something is small if it has none of these things. A little perfection is large for us. A large thing without beauty or truth is small for us. A creative seed is greater than a mountainous lump. Hence the invisible things are the smallest and the highest things amongst us. If a thing, a quality, an art, a gesture, a form becomes so refined and pure as to become invisible then it has ascended into the eternal.

'On the whole, big things are small for us. Great fame, great visibility, great temporal power are the easiest things for us to accomplish, according to our way. Hence we deem them small, and not worthy of our efforts.

'The most difficult thing for us is to do things which achieve permanence in the higher universe, and which are unseen, and can never therefore be destroyed. Our highest acts of creativity are in the empty spaces, in the air, in dreams, in unseen realms. There we have our cities, our castles, our greatest books, our great music, our art, science, our truest love, our fullest sustenance. If you are lucky you will partake of this higher condition, and delight in its power that transcends all boundaries.

'And sometimes – very rarely – but sometimes nonetheless, our highest creative acts, our highest playfulness, our self-overcoming, our purest art, our ascending songs, by some mysterious grace transcend so many boundaries and enter so many realms that we occasionally astonish even the gods.

'The best things in the world dwell in the realm of pure light, from where they spread their influence to all corners of the universe, to stones and men and worms, and even to stars and the dead and to angels. We are learning to be masters of the art of transcending all boundaries. We are learning to go beyond the illusion that is behind illusion.

'And even our way and our discoveries are still young in all their possibilities. We wake every day in a state of absolute humility and joyfulness at all that lies possible before us.

'Therefore we have no fame. We live quietly, as if within a sacred flame, and no one outside this island knows we exist. In our silence we dedicate ourselves to the perfection of our spirits, consecrated to serving the highest forces in the universe.

'We do not want to be remembered, or praised. We only want to increase the light, and to spread illumination.'

BOOK EIGHT

BOOK FOUR

One

He listened deeply to the silence speaking, till the silence itself changed. Something else took its place, a mood of expectation. He looked about him. The banners and buntings of the invisible city guild remained still. The trumpets and flutes were silent. A higher glow had entered the hall. He couldn't explain its source.

Then he heard his female guide say something to him. She said it three times before he heard. Then there was a long pause before he understood. And when he understood he became confused.

'You can only receive what you already have. You can only be given what you've already got,' she said, gently.

Still confused, he was about to speak when she touched him again. The effect of her touch was to make him intensely conscious of the fact that he was the focus of the expectant mood in the hall.

'Your moment has come,' she said, sweetly. 'You are being summoned to the stage.'

'But what for?' he asked, when he recovered from his confusion.

'For having got here,' she replied kindly. 'Go, and you will find out.'

And so, with much trepidation, he rose and climbed the

stairs to the stage. When he got on stage he noticed that both sides of the stage wall were composed of glowing mirrors. He was surprised that he hadn't noticed them before. Then it occurred to him that they weren't there before.

Within the mirrors, there were worlds and realms and dazzling existences. The things he glimpsed filled him with a shining terror. He tried not to look into the mirrors again.

He stood near the table closest to the edge of the stage, and he could feel the illuminated presence of the invisible masters behind him. He could also sense the uplifting effect of the colours and symbols on the banners. He felt the stoic rectitude of the invisible city guild, and the benevolent patience of the master musicians.

While he stood there a glass of water appeared mysteriously before him. He drank the water, and the glass was retrieved back into invisibility. Something cleared in his head. The clarity within him felt amazing, as if he had been given a new consciousness. The silence became deeper in the hall. It was a silence so clear he felt the doors of a higher realm had been opened. When he looked around he was amazed to see how truly vast the hall was, and he was awestruck by the sheer collective force of the invisible congregation.

And then, to his horror, he found himself in two places at the same time. He was still on the stage, in the hall, surrounded by the dazzling Invisibles, his mind in darkness. And yet, simultaneously, he was at the threshold of the great hall, beneath the arches, flooded in an ineffable light. The light was so universal that he couldn't see.

He stood in the utter darkness of light, at the threshold, under the arch, in deep silence, when he heard again the question he hadn't answered three times before. But this time the question had changed and the voice asking it was angelic.

'WHAT IS THE PURPOSE OF INVISIBILITY?'

Again silence weighed down his mind. But as he stood there, trembling in his inability, he felt the presence of his third guide and, without thinking, replied:

'PERFECTION.'

The lights became brighter, dissolving him in their deeper darkness. And the voice, more urgent, more seraphic, said:

'WHAT IS THE DREAM OF THE INVISIBLES?'

The silence that swelled in his mind made him soar into the edges of the light, flailing in the air. He was helpless and stricken with terror. But before he started to scream, the spirit of his second guide came to him and, with his heart beating faster under the mystery of his own clarity, he cried:

'TO CREATE THE FIRST UNIVERSAL CIVI-LISATION OF JUSTICE AND LOVE.'

After a brief silence, he heard strains of music. Then he saw, briefly, a faun playing on a flute. It played notes of such heartbreaking beauty that he started to weep. Then the music ceased, and the vision disappeared. The light and the darkness were now one.

And the voice, quieter now, almost inaudible, as if a deity was speaking with the register of the wind in the tall grass, said:

'WHAT IS THE MYSTERY OF THE BRIDGE?'

Lost in the perfect equality of darkness and light, of silence and sound, he wandered in the cool spaces of the question. Not afraid anymore, but brimming with joy, he felt the presence of his first guide. And, with a smiling voice, he replied:

'CREATIVITY, AND GRACE.'

At that moment he was overcome with light, flooded with

a supernal intelligence. He could feel the appreciation of the Invisibles. He could feel the warm brilliance of their smiles. It was like a faint golden mist in the hall, a fragrance of sunlight. He became as a child.

Two

A moment before he saw the congregation of the Invisibles as a host of luminous beings in vaporous white, he saw her mighty wings. He caught his breath. As if in a sublime dream, momentary as a vision of heaven, he saw her again, hovering above everything, conferring her benediction on all who are under her protection. He saw again – the liminal archangel of invisibility.

And as he stood there on the platform, dimly aware of the curious nature of his destiny, the most wonderful thing happened. He noticed something stirring within the mirror. And out of the mirror came a unicorn with a diamond horn. Before he could breathe, the unicorn trotted towards him silently. Then it stopped, and turned its mesmeric eyes upon him. Its horn was pointed heavenward.

Lost in the hypnotic eyes of the unicorn, he heard a sweet and primeval voice in the air say:

'Because your heart is pure you have found without seeking, overcome without knowing that you overcame, and arrived here when all who have tried have failed. You were born invisible. For anyone to get here they must, one way or another, come through your condition. There is no other way.'

When the voice ceased he felt, quite suddenly, as if he were in a shining place of silver, where all the known laws were different.

Then the unicorn, shimmering in an emerald light, trotted away from him gracefully and went out through the other mirror, leaving the air tinged with its mysterious philosophies.

Three

It came as a shock to him that as he looked into the glowing mirror, he could no longer see himself. He was not reflected there. However, just before he started to scream in mortal terror, he suddenly felt calm. He felt at one with the unknown happiness of the universe. He had become one of the Invisibles.

It seems odd and beautiful that he who had left home in search of the secret of visibility should have found a higher invisibility, the invisibility of the blessed.

All Orion/Phoenix titles are available at your local bookshop or from the following address:

Littlehampton Book Services
Cash Sales Department L
14 Eldon Way, Lineside Industrial Estate
Littlehampton
West Sussex BN17 7HE
telephone 01903 721596, *facsimile* 01903 730914

Payment can either be made by credit card (Visa and Mastercard accepted) or by sending a cheque or postal order made payable to *Littlehampton Book Services*.
DO NOT SEND CASH OR CURRENCY.

Please add the following to cover postage and packing

UK and BFPO:
£1.50 for the first book, and 50p for each additional book to a maximum of £3.50

Overseas and Eire:
£2.50 for the first book plus £1.00 for the second book and 50p for each additional book ordered

----

BLOCK CAPITALS PLEASE

name of cardholder ....
....

address of cardholder ....

....

....

....

postcode ....

delivery address
(if different from cardholder)

....

....

....

postcode ....

☐ I enclose my remittance for £ ....

☐ please debit my Mastercard/Visa (delete as appropriate)

card number ⬚⬚⬚⬚⬚⬚⬚⬚⬚⬚⬚⬚⬚⬚⬚⬚

expiry date ⬚⬚⬚⬚

signature ....

prices and availability are subject to change without notice